Through
the
Ruins of Midnight

Colin Campbell

Pen Press Publishers

First published in Great Britain
Pen Press Publishers Ltd
39-41 North Road
London N7 9DP

ISBN 1 904754-54-6
A catalogue record for this book is available
from the British Library

Printed and bound in Great Britain

Cover design by Jacqueline Abromeit

For Mum and Dad,
without whom I wouldn't be here.

...and my wife Karen,
without whom there wouldn't be any point.

For Mick Habergham, working the nightshift was the best thing about being a policeman. He enjoyed the peace and tranquillity of the midnight hours, when the world was asleep and patrol work simple. Sunday night should have been an easy shift but, as his mind wrestled with divorcing Angela, tonight would be anything but quiet.

From the mad knifeman of the Hill Top Hostel to the most inept suicide attempt at the House of Pain, Mick would encounter all manner of obstacles to a peaceful night. If it wasn't Marak Vargo, or Booger Smith, it would be the family party gone wrong at Chagrin Avenue, or the tragic pensioners of Maple Court. That was if he survived the battle at the Alex Public House.

Midnight ruined so many lives. Tonight one of them would threaten Mick's own. If he wanted to enjoy a happy retirement he would first have to walk through fields of heartache and survive the ruins of midnight.

FIRST TOUR

Sunday: 22.35 hrs

Mick Habergham didn't know this would be his last shift when he swung the patrol car into Pelham Terrace. He knew it was the last night of the week and he was due two days off, but other than that he still had four years left to retirement. The way his stab vest was irritating his neck, retirement couldn't come too soon. But tonight? No, he wasn't expecting that.

"What's the number again?"

Andy Scott looked across at his partner and sighed.

"How long you been in this job, Ham?"

That was Mick's nickname. Ham. He was a big man at six feet three and slightly overweight. Considering how much he ate it was surprising he wasn't as big as a house side, prompting Andy to rename him Hamburger instead of Habergham. Not exactly an anagram but close enough for the police canteen. Most of the shift hadn't realised that renaming Shania Twain, Shiny Twat, wasn't an anagram either but it always got a laugh. So, Hamburger it was, and since policemen like to shorten everything it became Ham.

"Long enough to forget the bloody house number," Ham said.

"Seventy-nine."

Ham flicked the headlights to full-beam and the cobbled street came into sharp relief. There were two streetlamps but neither threw out much light. The four remaining houses were back-to-backs, the rest just piles of rubble, so that narrowed

3

down the search. In this part of town you were lucky if any of the streets survived at all and Pelham Terrace was a weedy, overgrown wasteland clinging onto life on the outskirts. At just gone half past ten on a Sunday night there were still a few lights on and music hammered out of the end house near the railway lines. It echoed back off the retaining wall that blocked the cul-de-sac and disguised the fact that there was a twenty-foot drop at the other side.

One night a burglar had been chased out of that house by an irate Greek carrying a machete, climbing over the wall to escape. The only piece of luck he had that night was that the Inter-City express had been cancelled, otherwise he would have been mashed to pulp instead of just breaking both legs. The Greek was glad too because he nearly climbed after him before remembering where he was. The trains had been keeping him awake for two years.

"Can't hear the dog barking, so that's a good sign," Ham said.

"You know it's just waiting for you."

"Yeh, well I'm still a probationer don't forget. You should go in first."

That wasn't strictly true because Ham had completed his two years' probation twenty-four years ago. With twenty-six done, he had more service than the rest of the shift put together but sometimes the police force did funny things to you. Like flopped you lower than whale shit at regular intervals. He had spent the last fifteen years as a Scenes of Crime Officer, coming out twelve months ago when the force civilianisation programme caught him. He'd escaped the tenure policy when the Chief Constable decided that SOCO was so specialised that the obligatory five-years-and-you-were-out didn't apply, but they got him with the flying leg sweep. Took the feet right from under him.

After fifteen years away from front line policing he needed extensive retraining and got none if it. Thrown in at the deep end he knew less than the rawest recruit and had to relearn everything he'd ever known, and then some. Computerisation, scrambled radios, Police and Criminal Evidence Act. And stab vests. Not to mention taped interviews and the complete re-vamping of the prosecution file system. No, it was a jungle out there and he was back at the bottom of the food chain. He had to ask about everything twice and even then he couldn't re-member it all. Including the house number.

"What was the number again?"

"Christ. Sixty-nine."

"Seventy-nine. Sixty-nine I'd remember."

He wound the window down to get a better look at the house numbers. There were none. The music battered its way into the car, some unintelligible garage music you could make without any talent or musical instruments. The air outside was as warm as the air in the car, giving no respite at all from the heat of the night. It made the stab vest even more uncomfort-able and he vowed to take it off after meal.

The car drifted along the street and Ham checked the win-dows for signs of life. This was the part of night duty he en-joyed, the voyeuristic aspect of life on the beat. Not peeping Tomming but looking through the windows into another world. Another life. It had always fascinated him as a child when he'd watched buses from his bedroom window at night. You could see them running across the valley and once it was dark their interiors stood out against the dappled streets. Inside that glowing tube were a dozen lives intermingled by that single journey, each one touching the other if only briefly. They were projected onto the world like anonymous movie stars on the silver screen.

On night patrol the same thing applied to the windows he passed. He was on the outside looking in, a dark presence pulling back the curtain on someone else's world. Some of those worlds he became involved with, even changed, like the one he was about to invade now, but how many went by un-touched? How many people did he meet without meeting, and how many lives did their lives touch? It was fascinating. In the cold dead hours of night you were God. Tonight however it was the warm dead hours and he still couldn't find a house number.

The street was long enough to have a number seventy-nine but three-quarters of the houses had been knocked down. God knows why because nothing had been built in their place, leaving an overgrown patch of weeds and rubble where the other fifty-odd homes had been. The surviving block of houses were at the far end near the retaining wall, four at the front and four at the back. The first house looked like a shit tip; its small paved yard strewn with building materials, a wheelbarrow, two shovels, a cement mixer, and an aluminium ladder that was chained to the drainpipe. It was the scruffiest house on the block and therefore most likely the one they were looking for.

Ham shone his Maglite at the door and could just make out a dirty squidge that was the number. Seventy-nine. Of course it was. Of all the houses to choose from, why pick a clean one when you could have a roach motel instead. Judging from what the complainant had said, this was par for the course.

After turning out from briefing, Alpha Two were sent to their first message of the evening before catching their breath. Dog bite. Complainant wants seeing before eleven o'clock. Ham struggled into his stab vest despite the heat of the night, settling for shirtsleeves instead of his Nato jumper. Andy loaded their bags into the boot and off they went. The report was three days old but there had been no free units to attend until now. That meant the poor fella was going to be pissed off as well as bruised.

As it turned out he was more pissed than pissed off. Both he and his wife were nursing glasses of red wine while the husband handed a sheet of homework back to his ten-year-old son. The son's extended forehead and curly blond hair reminded Ham of the *Village of the Damned*. While they waited for the lad to settle at his makeshift desk in the corner, Ham wondered what time the little devil went to bed? Maybe he had taken control of the adults like the kids in the film, ruling with minds so powerful that they had protruding foreheads and shocking blond hair. An identical boy, only a couple of years older, popped his head round the corner wearing a grandfather dressing gown from the 1950s. He was obviously the ringleader because he simply glared at his parents then left the room.

"Right."

The man set his stall out for a long tale. He leaned forward, skewering Ham with eyes that had already started to redden and lose focus. He jabbed a finger at Ham's knee. Ham disliked him at once and wasn't at all surprised that a dog had bitten him. He felt like biting him himself.

"Happened on Thursday night, picking my daughter up from babysitting."

Ham recoiled at the prospect of a daughter lurking somewhere in the house and prayed that, unlike her brothers, she looked more like the mother. That would be small consolation however, since her mother looked like an inebriated owl, with fish-eyes and glasses you could make a table top out of.

"Now I don't want any trouble down there, cos my daughter needs to go back and, well, the bloke takes a drink. Know what I mean?"

Ham knew what he meant but doubted he would be in the same league as these two. In that he was wrong.

"Came out to see I was all right and grabbed the dog lead. Got a bit mad when it jerked and nearly spilled his beer. I heard someone inside say, eh-up Marco, he'll be after suing us."

Andy glanced across at Ham and they both saw the claim form going in to Claims Direct or one of those accident hotlines that were advertised on TV.

"Someone at work said I should report it to the police so you've got a record. Bit right through my trousers and drew blood. Spent two hours at the hospital getting a jab."

Boy wonder interrupted.

7

"It was this kind of dog wasn't it, Daddy?"

He held a brass ornament of an Alsatian up for inspection. The look in his eyes made Ham look for voodoo pins and tufts of hair.

"Yes, son. Great big Alsatian. Took a chunk out of my leg."

He pulled the right leg of his trousers up above the calf. There were three small puncture marks and a slight bruise but nothing you could describe as a chunk missing. It mustn't have done his trousers any good though. The man read Ham's mind.

"Didn't leave a mark on my trousers. But I don't want any trouble. Got the impression they were Gyppo types. Fly-by-nights. Don't want them having a go at my daughter when she babysits round the back."

The finger prodded Ham's knee again. Ham was becoming convinced that the man deserved more than a good bite, when Andy stepped in and asked for the address. With calm professionalism he extracted the address, description of the dog, and the fact that a teenage girl had been walking the dog when Mr Prod came out of the alley. The temptation had proved too much and the dog lunged at him, taking its pound of flesh. The girl wasn't strong enough to hold it back, and there you go. Dog bite. Andy turned the whole thing around and Ham almost fell at his feet in praise.

"I can tell from talking to you that you don't want to go through with a full report. You know, photographs, doctors' statements, give evidence in court and all that. But what we can do…"

He leaned forward as if keeping a secret, suckering the man into believing this was for him.

"…is go round and have a word with this fella. We'll start by telling him that you don't want to make a complaint, which you could do, but just want him to be more careful with his dog."

"Yeh, that's right."

"It could bite someone younger," his wife chipped in. "A child."

"Yeh. We don't want that," Mr Prod said. Andy agreed.

"Of course not. If we can stop that from happening then we'll have achieved something. So, we'll tell him to keep the dog muzzled when it's out, and that you don't want to push the matter because you still need to go down there. That you don't want to make things awkward for your daughter, but just want them to be aware of the dangers."

"Yeh."

Now the man began to think this was his idea and felt proud of himself.

"I just want them to keep the dog under control. That's all."

Andy stood up and checked his watch. The man suddenly looked worried.

"You're not going round now are you? Wouldn't want him getting narked, because like I said," he tapped his watch. "At this time of night he'll have been on the beer. I think he spends most nights drinking."

Mr Prod didn't see the irony of saying this while knocking back his vin rouge.

"Don't worry," Ham said. "Like my colleague said, we won't let on that this is something you want to do. You simply had to report it to protect the children in the street."

A good start to the night. Not exactly inbred but definitely a strange family. Ham was just glad they escaped without having to see the daughter. Some nights when you were on patrol you could come across completely sane and reasonable human beings. Victims of crime, key-holders for burgled premises, or sensible crooks that threw their hands up when caught and yelled, "It's a fair cop, guv." On the evidence of their first call this wasn't going to be one of those nights.

Looking at the upended wheelbarrow and the ladders chained to the drainpipe, Ham knew the night was about to take a turn for the worse. The first of many lives he would interact with after seeing them through the window. If a man's eyes are the windows to his soul, then the windows of the night are the eyes into another world. On the other side of that glass was a complete set of lives, with their own histories and network of connections that Ham didn't even know existed. Before tonight was over, one of them would end his career.

79 Pelham Terrace

The Delbacaro family weren't so much failures as complete and utter failures. Every single venture Marco had undertaken, from chicken rustling to security guarding, had ended in disaster. The chicken he stole turned out to be a cockerel and the neighbour he stole it from heard it crowing every morning until the police arrived and took it back. The only reason he wasn't arrested was because the constable who attended was too embarrassed to put him on the arrest sheet.

No, Marco was a complete and utter fuck-up and the family followed suit. His wife, Melinda, was as blind as a bat but too vain to wear glasses; his two teenage daughters were both a few sandwiches short of a picnic, and his guard dog was about as vicious as Dale Winton. To compensate for these inadequacies the entire clan took to the bottle and it was the only thing they were successful at. They were however an extremely close family. The daughters were dating two cousins from the next street and the dog would fuck anything within reach, including Marco's leg. You couldn't get any closer than that. If either of the girls got married they wouldn't be playing the Wedding March but Duelling Banjos.

The window into their world opened onto the living room and it was a microcosm of their entire lives. A natural disaster of biblical proportions. Melinda couldn't see worth a damn, so how she managed to hang the wallpaper was a miracle but judging by the gaps in the pattern it was a very small miracle.

The gaudy flower design was criss-crossed with missing petals, dissected stalks, and gaping sections of bare plaster. The only consolation was there was so much junk stacked around the room that half the wallpaper was hidden anyway. Then there was the ceiling rose. Marco fingered his head at the thought of that.

Melinda had fitted the heavy plaster rose in a frenzy of home improvement that was about as successful as her wallpapering. The glue was strong enough; she just couldn't see where to apply it. She had pasted a six-foot section of ceiling before clambering onto a buffet balanced on the coffee table. The glue was so thinly spread that when she finally got the rose into position there was barely enough to hold it in place and, with the precarious balance, she had no leverage to force it home. The rose looked fine for a couple of days then it fell on Marco's head, knocking him out. Undeterred she refitted it twice and both times it had crowned her husband sending him to the casualty department.

The family sat around the living room on this warm Sunday evening and Marco touched his head without thinking. Trisha was sitting on the settee with cousin number one while her sister, Carla, sat on cousin number two's lap in the easy chair. There was a Freudian message there if you looked for it but Carla was only marginally easier than Trisha. The dog was easiness personified and Marco had to stop it fucking his leg again as he reached for his beer. Melinda sat cross-legged on the floor in front of the fire, as if it wasn't warm enough in here already.

"What you want to watch tonight?" Marco asked no one in particular.

He stood next to the fire and studied the piles of videotapes stacked against the walls. The alcoves on either side of the chimney breast were piled high with all manner of audio and visual treats. On the right was the Schwarzenegger collection, pre-recorded videos they'd picked up at boot sales and second-hand shops over the years. Next to them were dozens of home-taped videos. Every episode of *Star Trek*, five tapes of *Doctor Who*, including the William Hartnel original, and a selection of *Baywatch* videos. There were hundreds of audiocassettes, a mountain of CDs, and three cuddly toys that nobody remembered buying.

Somewhere beneath all this was a cracked Sony hi-fi that only worked three days a week, and a pair of dusty speakers. At least the speakers were the requisite six feet apart but the left hand one was hidden behind a four-foot plastic alien in a baseball cap and three box sets of *The X Files* videos. That section was more dangerous than the rest because it was the Mulder and Scully corner. The Delbacaros had not only taped every episode off the TV but also bought separate collections when they came out on sell-through video. In true money-grabbing fashion Fox then released some of the episodes as special editions including interviews with cast members, and again as ultimate collectors' editions including a couple more interviews and a stills gallery. There were also the box sets and finally the whole thing started again with the DVD editions. They didn't even own a DVD player.

Somewhere among the FBI's finest was the television, a tobacco stained relic of the post war era. The screen was so dirty that everything looked as if it was filmed in sepia and even if it was cleaned the tube was knackered, turning everyone into two-foot midgets with very wide heads. The Delbacaros weren't bothered. By the time it came to watching TV they were usually too drunk to notice, so the question was irrelevant but he asked it again anyway.

"What you want to watch tonight?"

"The dog shagging your leg."

Cousin number two shuck, shucked his hillbilly laugh. Carla snuggled her bundle into his lap and his pecker pinged up. Trisha giggled, as much at the surprised look on her cousin's face as what he'd said. You could have recited the telephone directory and she would giggle. She had a giggling sort of outlook on life, as if the wire on her serious side had come loose, shorting out the circuit. She wasn't sure if she was with the right cousin either and that made her laugh as well.

"Not funny, Trisha. Dog's supposed to be a guard dog. Should have chopped its nuts. It'd bite then."

"Leave my baby alone."

Melinda turned to stroke the dog. Marco turned on her.

"Ain't your baby. Them's your babies, and they're more on heat than he is."

Trisha giggled again and this time Carla smirked as well. She rubbed her bottom into her boyfriend's groin and he went cross-eyed. Marco sipped his beer and looked at the teetering pile of videos. Half a dozen posters of Mulder and Scully were pinned to the wall and they seemed to point him in that direction. *The X Files* wasn't his favourite show but he could watch that posh tart any time so it was probably the safest bet tonight. Melinda loved David Duchovny and the girls were too preoccupied anyway so he pulled a tape out of the season two box set. He spoke over his shoulder.

"Social books tomorrow. Whose turn is it to go to the post office?"

"Mine," Carla said.

Cousin number one offered to go with her.

"Been a lot of muggings lately."

Trisha bounced on his lap, forcing a grunt of pain.

"You're supposed to protect me, not her."

He looked hurt and turned her face toward his, displaying an intelligence that appeared beyond him.

"Honey, you know I only have eyes for you. But that money's for all of you. Gets stolen and you're all in the poor house. I feel I ought to contribute but my money goes to the folks. So, whoever goes to the post office, I should look out for them. It just ain't your turn, that's all."

Trisha soaked it up like she always did. Gullible as a fish in fish-stew.

"Ah, that's sweet of you."

She pecked him on the cheek and didn't notice Carla stop

rubbing cousin number two's groin. Melinda did though, showing insight that outweighed her lack of vision in the eyeball department. She saw a lot more than that as well.

"Ah fuck."

Marco struggled to get the cassette into the video. As hard as he pushed, the front loader wouldn't accept it and in that respect it was just like Melinda. No matter how hard he tried she wasn't interested in being porked any more. His foreplay techniques were no more successful with the video. The tape was rejected again, purring back out the front of the machine.

"It's already got one in," Carla said.

Marco bent to look but couldn't see past the entry flap.

"Press eject."

He did. There *was* already one in and in that way it was also similar to his wife who had been getting more than sausage from the local butcher for the past six months. *Deliverance* slid out of the hole and he popped *The X Files* in for sloppy seconds. More than he was likely to get from Melinda.

She, on the other hand, was concentrating on their daughters, Carla in particular. While she absent-mindedly stroked the dog, which had rolled onto his back with his legs in the air, settling for a hand job instead of mounting Marco's leg, her eyes scrutinised the girl as she settled back into her boyfriend's lap.

Melinda fell pregnant with Carla twelve months after meeting Marco and, despite being unemployed, he'd immediately proposed. Nineteen years ago he still had something of the knight-in-shining-armour about him, and not a little foreplay, stemming from his elevated position as head of security at the packaging plant. She had loved him then, although even she couldn't understand how he'd been promoted. The rest of the staff must have been real no-brainers.

They married in the summer and had Carla six months later, a happy accident they never regretted. Trisha was planned and came along two years later but it was Carla that Melinda had a deep affection for. They were so in tune that sometimes

15

they had the same thought simultaneously and it was just a case of who got the words out first. If her daughter was worried about something Melinda knew even before she asked for help. And unusually for a mother and daughter she did ask for advice whenever she needed it, Melinda giving it without bias. She might be blind but some things she could see pretty clear. Right now what she saw was trouble.

She took a swig of lager from a long-stemmed glass and didn't have to ask what the problem was. She'd been pregnant twice and could see the signs with her eyes closed, more accurate than a home pregnancy test. One thing she was certain of, the father wasn't cousin number two. The dog squirmed under her hand, wagging his tail and almost knocking her glass over. She grabbed it with both hands and didn't spill a drop, a sharp stab of panic cutting through her thoughts.

Marco squeezed onto the end of the settee, pushing Trisha into the corner, and the Twentieth Century Fox fanfare blared out of the TV – the speaker was almost as bad as the tube. A moth popped and spun around the light bulb, threatening to bring the ceiling rose down, and the soft flutter of wings sent a shiver down Melinda's spine. Maybe she had watched too many episodes of *The X Files* but sometimes she thought that horrible creatures came with a pair of wings. Not for her the simple beauty of a chaffinch or a sparrow, what she saw was an unpredictable beast with a beak and claws, and the ability to dart around your head when you least expected it. Bats were even worse, and moths were right up there with them. Horrible furry fucks that scared her to death.

The X Files theme came on, its gentle lilting tones soothing her, and thoughts of who'd been sleeping with her daughter drifted away on a cloud of lager fumes and Mulder and Scully.

The dog padded round the living room looking for someone else to pester, considering Trisha for a moment, then settling on Carla, who sometimes took him for his nightly walk. It sat in front of her and lifted a paw in greeting, trying to persuade her with a swish of the tail that caused a stronger draft than the mobile fan burring in the corner. Carla's mind was elsewhere though.

She had caught a glimpse of something in her mother's eye and knew that before the night was through she would have to tell her what she probably already knew. That she was pregnant. The thought of confiding in her mother didn't worry her, being pregnant wasn't the worst thing that could happen to a Delbacaro, but telling her who the father was did. There was enough family tension to retune a grand piano, the sisters providing most of it. No, that was going to be hard. Telling her father would be impossible.

Marco had a strict moral code when he was sober, even if the Delbacaro code bore no relation to the accepted standards of a mongrel country, and a fuse that was shorter than a ten-second timer. When he'd been drinking, that fuse became an instant detonator, so it would have to be her mother tonight and hope he didn't find out for a few days. The dog wagged its tail but she ignored it. Stupid mutt had almost blown the story last week and she was in no mood to remember the shock of that moment. Only quick thinking and a devious nature had saved the day. That and the fact that the dog had a bite like a wet kipper.

Mulder and Scully had a secret meeting with the cigarette-smoking man on the TV and the plastic alien in front of the speaker stared across the room. Sometimes Carla thought the alien noticed more around the Delbacaro household than the rest of them put together, bearing more than a passing resemblance to the inbred cousins the girls were dating. Both had vacant expressions and looked good in baseball caps.

The dog wagged its tail, and the moth bumped its way around the bulb, and Mulder and Scully continued their investigations into the paranormal. All was right with the world. The knock on the door shattered all that, not only jerking them into action but also provoking a guilty look from Carla. Nobody liked the police coming round and that was definitely a policeman's knock.

*

Ham waited for the bark that accompanied most of his door knocking and was surprised when it didn't come. Considering they were here because "The Hound of the Baskervilles" had savaged Mr Prod, that was even more surprising. He glanced over his shoulder at Andy who stood two paces back near the gate, keeping the wheelbarrow between him and any beast that might come out of the front door.

"No reply," Ham said quickly. "Right let's go."

"It's the last night. You know God isn't going to be that kind to you on your last night."

Andy was probably right but still nobody answered the door. Ham knocked again. He knew he couldn't get away with leaving a Form 150 because they had both seen the family watching TV as they'd got out of the car. The man and the woman were sitting apart but the two girls they spied were as close to their boyfriends as you could get. No sign of the dog though. Someone could be out walking it but Ham didn't think there was anyone missing from The Waltons inside.

The windows don't lie. Mostly what you see is what you get.

Ham had come to accept that over the years. Of all the windows he'd looked through in his career, the majority showed exactly what he was getting himself into, the scene played out on that opaque screen as clear as anything at the Odeon. A little old lady upset at having her handbag snatched; a violent domestic between a drunken husband and his even drunker wife; the deadly stillness of a sudden death. Of course, the films at the local cinema were make-believe, concocted at great expense so that everything you saw *was* a lie, but on the budget of your everyday victim there were no special effects or optical illusions. What you saw was truly what you got. On the surface anyway.

Ham knocked louder, giving the door his number-one policeman's knock. Not his polite *I'm-sorry-to-disturb-you*
knock, but the *come-on-I-haven't-got-all-day* knock. The
knock that was reserved for warrant enquiries when you knew
the suspect was inside, or the harassment warning knock where
you wanted to establish authority straight away. Or the *your-
dog-just-bit-an-innocent-man* knock where the dog owner
was sitting watching TV. Whatever you called it there was no
mistaking it for your maiden aunt. When that knock went down
there was definitely a policeman at the door.

"Coming," an agitated voice called from inside.

Ham thought he heard the suggestion of a muffled bark.
Two bolts were drawn back then a key turned and the door
swung inwards throwing yellow light into the street. The heat
hit him like a tidal wave, robbing him of his voice for a second.
An angry man glared at him and Ham knew that Mr Prod had
been right, drink was definitely an issue here.

"Sorry to bother you at this time," Ham said, contradicting
the knock he'd used. "It's about your dog. Can we come in for
a minute?"

The man stood in the doorway and for a moment Ham
didn't think he was going to let them in, then he stood to one
side and grunted an "All right," as he waved them into the
lounge. Ham went in first but Andy let Mr Angry follow before bringing up the rear. Even with a job as simple as this you
shouldn't let an angry man stand behind both of you.

Heat from the fire drained Ham as soon as he passed through
the door and he cursed the stab vest under his breath. It was
definitely coming off after meal. He wiped a hand across his
forehead and smiled at the woman sitting cross-legged in front
of the fire.

"Phew. Lost six pounds already. You do know it's an In-
dian summer don't you?"

The girls sniggered and one of the boys yuck-yucked. The
woman looked up.

"Want me to turn it down?"

"Please. Otherwise I'll need smelling salts in a minute."

"Sorry."

The woman leaned over and turned the gas down. Ham took a minute to cool, scanning the scene before he spoke. The man who let them in was nursing a glass of beer and the woman near the fire had a long-stemmed glass. Two attractive girls sat with their boyfriends, each with a bottle of Budweiser beside the armrest. The picture of domestic bliss was only missing one thing and that thing lunged round the coffee table before Ham could get out of the way, all snarling teeth and wagging tail. The wagging tail didn't fool him; this was the Hound of the Baskervilles.

"Come here you little softy."

At first Ham thought the woman was talking to him. She put her glass on the table and wrestled the beast's head between her ample breasts. The tail wagged faster and the dog pointed half an inch of rhubarb from between its legs.

"Softy, softy."

Her words belied the fact that part of it was anything but soft. Ham pointed at the dog.

"Exhibit A. It's the dog we've come about."

One of the girls tensed and the woman took the dog's head into protective custody between her breasts. The man just glared.

"It's nothing to worry about. Just about last Thursday when your dog bit the fella outside. Now he isn't making a complaint, let's get that straight up front. But he thought he needed to report it. Doesn't want to fall out with anyone since his daughter babysits round the back."

The girl on the chair shifted uneasily but her boyfriend didn't seem to mind. Mr Angry drank his beer and continued to glare while the dog-protection woman almost suffocated the pooch between her breasts. Its tail wagged so violently it nearly knocked her glass over. Ham nodded at the table.

"That dog gets any more excited you're going to have an empty glass."

"Thanks."

She moved the glass out of tail's reach. Ham looked warily at the dog, waiting for the barking lunge that his uniform usually provoked. Andy kept one step behind him, using Ham as a shield. So far the dog hadn't barked and it looked like it would rather fuck him than bite him. Mulder and Scully engaged in a shouting match with some minor official on the TV, distracting Ham from the issue at hand.

"Could you just turn that down for a minute?"

The man did, then took another swig of his beer.

"Thanks. Whose dog is it? I just need some details."

"Mine."

The woman saw Ham's reluctance to come near the dog. "Only bites Asians."

"Does that mean if I don't black up I'll be all right?"

"Doesn't like 'em. Asians."

"Well, the fella it bit was white. No turban or anything."

The girls sniggered and Huckleberry Finn yuck-yucked again. All he needed was a piece of straw in his teeth and the picture would be complete. Now that Ham thought about it, the two boys did bear a certain family resemblance and they didn't look too dissimilar from Mr Angry either. Ham was beginning to think that this particular window was keeping something back. The dog came up for air and the woman turned her gaze to the tall policeman. It was the first time he noticed that both her eyes didn't work in sync. Banjo music began to play in the back of his mind.

"And what's your name please?"

Melinda gave her details then Marco followed suit. Ham wasn't interested in the love twins or their beaus. The dog was called Sabre and, now the strangers had been accepted into the family, it slinked towards Ham with its tail still wagging between its legs. The head bowed and its eyes were filled with sorrow and Ham had to admit that it didn't look like the kind of dog that would attack an innocent bystander. It sniffed the air in front of his legs then dodged back when Ham moved

21

his pocket book, tail wagging all the time.

Encouraged, Ham offered the back of his hand and Sabre licked it twice then retreated. When Ham didn't bite, it came back and licked some more, its tail back to full wag status. It thumped against the coffee table and before he could warn Melinda again the long-stemmed glass was knocked over. Amber liquid spilled across the glass top and Melinda exploded.

"Fuckin stupid dog."

Sabre jumped and scurried into the kitchen. Melinda mopped the drink with a tissue then drank the last from the glass. Andy stepped forward, emboldened by the dog's yellow streak. He followed on from his speech to Mr Prod.

"Like we said, the man doesn't want to make a complaint but we can't have your dog biting people in the street can we?"

Marco bristled.

"Shouldn't have come running out of the back alley then should he?"

"Is that what happened?"

Andy let Marco think he was in charge.

"Just came running out."

This was a slightly different story than Mr Prod's but Ham was used to that. He had come to expect opposite versions of events from victims and offenders. He dealt with an assault once that occurred on the complainant's doorstep when, if you believed his version, six Asians got out of a black 4X4 and beat him up for no reason. On interview later, the offender said he only had one friend with him and they called on the complainant to settle an accident claim. He said he was not angry that the man had refused to pay for the last two weeks and merely wished to talk about it.

So, on the one hand, you had six Asians committing an unprovoked assault and on the other a man who just wanted to talk about the £800's worth of damage to his car. Neither threw the first punch and yet both did, depending on who you believed. Somewhere in between lay the truth and Ham sensed it even though he couldn't prove it. The Asians had come round to sort out payment, but not peacefully, and the man had refused to pay because he wasn't insured. Also he was pissed and even less likely to see reason, so he'd thrown the first punch after voices were raised. Then he got the crap kicked out of him and reported it to the police. QED.

Now it was time to find out just how different the dog attack was from the other side of the fence. Ham watched Andy do his work.

"What time was this?"

"About ten or half ten."

With careful questioning Andy got the story out of him. It differed from the original report in several ways but was essentially the same. The dog was being walked. A man got bitten. And it happened last Thursday night. That was as much as the two stories agreed. According to Marco Delbacaro, the dog was being walked on a lead near the front of their house when a man ran out of the passage. Sabre snapped at him as he passed and bit his leg. Marco enquired about the leg and when it didn't seem too serious went back inside. End of story.

Ham sat on the chair arm and stroked the dog while Andy worked his magic. His eyes roamed the faces of the Delbacaros and pieced together his own version of the truth. One thing was for certain; Marco wasn't walking the dog that night. The look on Carla's face told him that. She listened to the story unfold with a face that was an open book; suspicion when Andy asked if the dog was on a lead; anxiety when her father wasn't sure; and relief when he said he'd been drinking and lost control when the dog lunged forward. The truth, or part of it, was as easy to detect as the stolen hen that was really a cockerel. It crowed the dawn and gave away its position so clearly that all the police had to do was walk in and uncover it. But Ham didn't think this little secret needed uncovering. Not tonight. There were more important crimes to deal with than a bite from a frightened dog, or the infidelities of a teenage girl.

Anyway, they'd already agreed to let Marco off with a

warning and Mr Prod didn't want any action taking beyond that so what did it matter who was walking the dog? Ham stood up as Andy finished talking, satisfied that the contents of this particular window had been exhausted. The night was young and there were plenty more to explore.

Sunday: 23.25 hrs

The stab vest rubbed Ham's Adam's apple as they patrolled the streets north of town. Not a bad start to the shift, two inbred families and a gay dog, and they hadn't even met the family from hell yet. He wound the window down to let the air circulate but it didn't cool the patrol car, simply blowing his hair around and annoying Andy.

"Shut the window for Christ's sake. It's blowing a gale over here."

"You know, for someone of your tender years you've got no blood at all."

"Age has nothing to do with it. If I want fresh air I'll ask for a foot beat."

This was nonsense of course because there were hardly enough officers to cover all three cars, never mind put someone out on foot and even on Sunday night doing foot patrol on your own wasn't safe. Andy tapped his temple.

"Senile dementia, that's your problem."

"Better than penile dementia. The way you carry on your chances of surviving thirty years are slim."

Andy had practically started his own in-breeding programme on the shift, having porked any female member who would have him at one time or another. He steadfastly ignored Ham's golden rule; never sleep with anyone you work with, it will bring nothing but grief. That was something Ham had never done, even when relations with Angela had been at their worst.

Now that there were serious decisions to be made he had no intention of complicating matters further.

He turned into the Persimmon Homes Estate and looked through the windows as they drifted past at patrol speed. Patrol speed for Ham that was; for Andy it was considerably faster. Ham couldn't understand how Andy expected to see anything as they flashed through the night. For Ham's first six months back on the streets he suffered whiplash every time Andy spun the car round to follow a suspect vehicle. No, this was much better and as a bonus he could see into the houses they passed. Through the windows that looked back at him.

Even at this time of night there were still plenty of lights on. That would be true right through the night on the rough side of town. He sometimes wondered how they could stay up all night, breaking the back of midnight then grinding out the hours till dawn, but they did. In the potholed streets of the Cowgill estate there were more who stayed up than went to bed. Most of the ones who were out were busy trying to get into someone else's house. When prison beckoned they were happy to leave their untidy palaces for a six-month break.

That untidy thought brought Angela to mind. Despite being married to her for two years, he sometimes thought she belonged here rather than at home with him. The mess she left behind was only part of the problem and would have to be addressed soon. Maybe tonight. The moment for decisive action had passed long ago but tonight was the last straw.

The windows of the Persimmon estate were cleaner than those on Cowgill, so neat and tidy he could have moved in right away and let Angela fend for herself. The problem was she couldn't fend for herself and he knew it. The responsibility weighed heavy on his shoulders, a thousand straws that individually weighed nothing but together... Creak.

The house on the left was a modern detached with integral garage. By detached the builders meant at least two feet apart, but the newness of the building was complemented by the fresh look within. A bedroom window was lit, curtains drawn, but the living room was open for inspection. The lights were on and curtains open to the world. From the shadows of night Ham soaked up the beauty of that room's simplicity. He slowed the car to a crawl.

Wall-mounted brass fittings illuminated the alcoves and the orange glow of the walls evoked Greek villas on a sunny afternoon. Yellow throw cushions padded out the ochre settee and two simple but colourful paintings hung on opposite walls. The bay window begged you to come in. Ham found himself hoping the next call would come from here, knowing that was wishing tragedy on whoever lived there. The police didn't bring good news. If you won the lottery you asked for Linda Lusardi not PC Plod.

The car droned on. Three doors down another light was on. Once again the living room was an open book, an erotic experience as potent as watching strangers make love. This time there was movement downstairs, an elderly couple watching the late night movie on Channel Four. The man brought a tray from the kitchen, standing out against the white walls with pressed flowers decorating the alcoves. The main lights were off but a standard lamp spread light from one corner, blue and white light flickering as the TV played in the other. It was a cosy scene and Ham wondered what their names were? What their life consisted of behind these clean sharp windows?

"Ham? You awake?"

Andy was looking at him with an amused smile.

"Course I am."

"It's just that if you go any slower we'll be going backwards."

Ham nearly offered Andy the wheel, then thought better of it. Andy nodded ahead.

"It's a good job the road's straight. You haven't looked where you're going for the last ten minutes."

"You are not getting the wheel until after meal."

"Poetic justice from the poet."

Ham smiled at the irony in Andy's voice.

"Yeh well, when you drive I spend half my time looking like that lass in *The Exorcist*. Head on back to front."

"So long as you don't vomit pea soup. What did Barney mean about the tank door yesterday?"

Ham laughed at the memory. Barney had been in the job four years when Ham joined and had showed him the ropes during his formative years. Barney was a veteran detective in the Stolen Vehicle Squad and they'd run into him last night in the cells. The tank door incident cropped up whenever they met. That and the footprint on the drunk's chest.

"Long story from long, long ago."

"In a galaxy far, far away?"

"No. Just another town."

They reached the end of a cul-de-sac and Ham turned the car round, heading back past the windows he found so fascinating. He ignored them this time, his mind drifting back to safer times. Or were they? The tank door would suggest otherwise.

"So, what was he talking about?"

"Maybe you shouldn't know while I'm driving."

"Maybe I should if you're driving."

"If you insist," Ham said and started talking.

*

Barney Koslowski was an overweight policeman long before it became fashionable to be an overweight policeman. He liked his beer and he liked his women, and neither sat very well with his wife at the time. He was also a dyed-in-the-wool good copper with so much practical experience that he didn't need to know chapter-and-verse about the laws he upheld, his nose simply lead him and the rest followed. He could sniff out a crook at a hundred paces.

He was young and keen when Ham met him, with an old head on his shoulders. He was twenty-five going on fifty, with one of those infectious laughs that got everyone on his side

from the Superintendent down. He was destined for great-
ness. If he could keep out of trouble.

They worked together at Clayton Wood Police Station, a
single-cell cop shop with a custody area the size of a bathroom and a CID office above the integral garage. The front
office was straight out of *Heartbeat*, a craggy affair with two
wooden desks, a telephone, and barred windows that Houdini
wouldn't be able to get through. During the day there was
enough light to lift the gloom but not enough to read by. The
solitary bowl-light hanging on a chain from the ceiling pretended to help but didn't. A bit like the sergeant who ran the
office as if the money came from his own pocket. Stationery
was kept under lock and key and you'd better have a damn
good reason if you wanted any.

Into this environment came a young and naïve Mick
Habergham.

After eighteen months of watching and learning, the only
thing he knew for sure was that he would never be anything
like Barney Koslowski. Barney had a knack for sniffing out
crime that became legendary and was already a veteran even
though he only had four years in. He could walk down the
street and crooks would drop out of the trees like leaves on an
autumn day. It was uncanny.

One particular nightshift he had parked up and gone walka-
bout in the student district, checking the back doors of the
Chinese Take-away and The Pizza Parlour. Both premises
had been burgled three times in the last six months and Barney
had an itch that needed scratching. When he got those itches
you'd better take notice because the shit was about to hit the
fan.

It wasn't the Chinkies or the Italians who got hit that night
but a Polish refugee who had set up his own hi-fi shop. He
bought and sold anything from portable record players to new-
fangled eight-tracks, a piece of hardware he didn't think stood
a chance against the smaller cassette players. 'Poles Apart'
was on the main road at Hyde Park Corner with a small alley-

way down one side. It didn't lead anywhere but the owner liked the flower border beneath the side window. The window was barred and wired.

Barney found out by chance as he strolled past the mouth of the alley. That itch became unbearable and he paused with his back to the shop. Silence. At three in the morning there wasn't any traffic – unlike these days when Hyde Park Corner was the hub of the student universe and was never quiet. He sniffed the air, senses questing for the cause of that itch. He looked at the selection of record players and scratched LPs in the window and didn't give the alley a second glance.

Something must have drawn him there however and the itch transformed itself into a bursting need for a pee. He walked up the alley far enough to be away from the road and stepped over the low wall onto the flower border. The leaves rustled as he settled down, unzipped his fly, and stared blankly at the barred window while he relieved himself. The window was secure, no sign of interference, and there was no light on inside. He shook off the drips, mindful of the adage that more than three shakes was a wank, and the leaves rustled again. The itch returned. It ran up his legs like a rash and even before the burglar broke cover Barney had the handcuffs out.

"Fuck."

The man couldn't hold his breath any more.

"Fucking fuckety fuck."

His head and shoulders were soaked with piss and henceforth Barney was known as the Bobby who pissed on crime. To Mick he also became known as the man who let him practice driving even before he got his permit.

In hindsight, letting Mick drive around Potternewton playing-field at two in the morning wasn't the thing to do after three days of torrential rain, but on that night the rain held off, and the rugby pitch seemed okay from the road. In fact it was okay at first and when Mick got behind the wheel there were no problems. The battered Marina flew across the ten-yard line and round the home team posts without incident. Thus emboldened, he strayed onto the neighbouring football pitch and that's where he came a cropper.

The handbrake turn and sudden burst of acceleration sank the wheels to the axles and stuck the car solid. The more he revved the deeper they sank and before Barney could stop him Mick had buried the car up to the doors. After a few choice words Barney took over, forcing Mick to walk round up to his ankles in mud while Barney slid across the seat. No matter how carefully he tried, the car wouldn't budge and he had to call for the divisional Range Rover to drag them out.

Unfortunately the traffic man on duty thought he could drive onto the field, hook up, and tow them away without realising how soft the ground was. Result. A patrol car and a Range Rover stuck in the mud. The Force recovery truck was called out to throw them a line from the main road. It took three hours to get them out.

Barney never let on that Mick had been driving. Mick liked to think that showed incredible loyalty but it was more likely the fact that Barney would have lost his driving permit. It was three months before he let Mick drive again. You would have thought he'd learned his lesson after the Potternewton fiasco but no, persistence was Mick's middle name, and this time he gave Barney a real headache.

Patrolling the backstreets and shopping precincts was one thing but the place to find thieves abandoning their stolen cars was off the beaten track. There was nowhere more off the beaten track than Meanwood Ridge. A broad footpath ran from the houses on the hill all the way down the valley to the industrial estate near town. In summer it was the haunt of walkers and lovers. In the winter it was a barren footpath that was too cold to walk and at night was positively dangerous. One of the Yorkshire Ripper's victims had been found barely alive not far from the bottom. It was a magnet for all sorts of illegal activities. Including torching stolen cars.

Once the sun had gone down Barney often drove the length of the path, which was just wide enough for a patrol car, dropping down the gentle slope towards the beck and the Wood-cutter's Arms. On this particular late turn, with just over an hour to finishing time, he let Mick drive. That wasn't his main mistake. He should have checked the weekly bulletin instead of going on instinct as usual because then he would have known that the footpath had changed.

At nine o'clock the patrol car crested the ridge, its head-lights shooting out into the valley before dropping to show the winding path. Mick was busy concentrating on the clutch/ac-celerator combination and Barney stared out of the side win-dow at the treetops. They were already heading down the slope before Mick realised something was wrong.

The path had disappeared.

He slammed the brakes on but the gravel wouldn't let him stop, the car sliding sideways until it rested at the edge of the abyss. The headlights cut a path across the grassy slope, pick-ing out the nearest trees but shedding no light whatsoever on the drop beside them. Mick slipped the car into reverse and slowly edged backwards, straightening their line before pulling forward again. A single railway sleeper lay across the path. In the shadows beyond it was another then another. The path had been dug out and stepped using sleepers to edge the ris-ers.

So far they were in a bit of a pickle but nothing too drastic. What Mick did next put them beyond that and into serious shitsville. He tried reversing up the slope but the gravel was having none of it then, before Barney could stop him, he drove over the step in the hope that it wasn't too deep. It was. Thunk. The car grounded on the heavy wood. Dabbing the accelera-tor only produced a scream of tyres and spitting gravel and didn't move the car at all. Forward or reverse, it didn't make any difference. The car was stuck. Barney cursed.

"Aw fuck. Gimme the wheel."

Once again Mick trudged around the car as Barney slid over the seat. The wheels spun and the gravel flew, and the car didn't move an inch. Well, that was a lie because it did move, but sideways towards the edge of the slope, which ran steep as a ski slope down to the beck.

"Aw fuck," Barney said again.

"Sorry."

"Sorry my fucking arse. Look at the time."

It was half-past nine and they were due off at ten. Barney thought for a moment then told Mick to get out. They both went to the back of the car and tried to lift and slide it towards the edge of the sleeper. It moved a foot then stopped. More fuck, fuck, fucking from Barney and then he called for Bravo Two to rendezvous at the top of the ridge. Luckily Pete Blakeney was crewing Bravo Two and if anyone could shift the back of the patrol car it was him. He could rip telephone books in half and bend iron bars in his teeth, and he was a very good friend of Barney Koslowski.

Half an hour later they had shifted the car off the sleeper and onto the grassy bank. The only problem now was getting it down the hill to rejoin the path below the steps without tumbling into the beck. One short-lived attempt proved it wasn't going to reverse back up the hill, almost sliding backwards down the slope to oblivion. The incline was too steep to simply drive parallel to the path.

So, in a hilarious precursor to the tank door incident, Barney drove carefully down the hill with two policemen hanging out of the open passenger doors like a pair of motorcycle sidecar racers, balancing the weight of the car against the bulk of Mick Habergham and the greater bulk of Pete Blakeney. Afterwards Barney vowed never to let him drive again, and he didn't. Until the night of the alarm, and the tree branch, and the one and only tank door. It became the staple diet of any encounter with Barney for the rest of Ham's career, and the story Andy Scott wanted to hear now.

Mick was single-crewed on the first set of nights after getting his permit. It was late November and the trees had finally shed their coats of leaves in favour of the naturists' way, naked as the day they were born. In the case of the oak and sycamore around Clayton Wood Police Station that meant sin-ewy branches and spindly fingers that made the night even colder, a stark reminder of just how near Christmas they were.

He checked the patrol car religiously before each shift as the manual insisted, testing the lights, then the indicators, and finally the blue lights and siren. Nobody tested the siren be-cause it made such a noise but Mick did, to the annoyance of the rest of the shift. By mid-week he'd been persuaded to forget the siren, Barney arguing that once it got past ten o'clock he could get anywhere he needed to with the blue flashing lights alone. Didn't want to be scaring the burglars off before he got there did he? Ham insisted on wearing his seat belt, a legacy of good driving practice, and actually felt unsettled if he drove anywhere without it.

Friday night was busy up until midnight when the evening's domestics had died down to the occasional rumble of discon-tent. By mealtime it was deader than the leaves piled along the country lanes. Two in the morning seemed a strange time to be eating doorstep sandwiches and playing cards but that's what Barney was doing when Mick entered the canteen. Los-ing as well, judging by his face. Pete Blakeney had once won twenty-five pounds on a single hand at three-card-brag. That was two weeks' food allowance for Mick, who was living in a bedsit at the time.

Barney and Mick had finished eating when the immediate came in, intruder alarm at Ashfield Cottage, Clayton Lane. Still in the throws of enthusiasm Mick lunged for the door like a pilot in The Battle of Britain. Too many episodes of *The Sweeney* for him to ignore the burst of adrenalin. Forget the paperwork, or the enquiries, or the school crossings, it was the emergencies that got him going.

Mick was first out of the car park, closely followed by Barney. Ashfield Cottage was two miles away along the tree-lined country lane and it was rich pickings for any burglar who tackled it. He was halfway there when he realised he hadn't put his seatbelt on but with Barney sniffing at his heals he ploughed on, taking the bends faster and faster. He rocked from side to side without the reassurance of the belt and, when he hit the sharp left-hander, he knew he couldn't make it. The patrol car lost its grip and barrelled to the other side of the road, slamming into a ditch. The driver's window shattered as a thick branch muscled its way into the safety cubicle, narrowly missing his face. Cold night air stung his eyes.

Barney flew past and slammed the brakes on. Adrenalin was pumping and there was still the alarm to get to. The burglars might be getting away. Mick's car was on its side in the ditch and the only way to get out was the passenger door. He flipped it open and it stood on its hinge like a peeled-back lid on a can of beans, or a tank hatch. Mick clambered onto the roof, which was really the side of the car, and dropped to the road. Barney flung his door open and Mick jumped in; then they were off to Ashfield Cottage, Barney laughing all the way.

It was a false alarm. After checking the premises they called it in and cancelled the dog. Before reporting the accident Barney drove back to the car and checked the damage. The driver's window was gone, an ugly grey branch filling the car. How it had missed Mick's face God only knew. Mick was shaking now, shock tweaking his system once the adrenalin rush subsided. A pair of wicked black skid marks led across the road, telling the world how fast Mick had been driving when he took the bend.

That's when Barney really showed his mettle. Forget being the thief-catcher extraordinaire, and forget taking the rap for sinking his patrol car in the mud, this was where he showed what real friends were for. He sat Mick down in his car then flung wedges of mud along two-thirds of the skid-mark's length, and then he drove over them two or three times at speed until they blended with the road. Only then did he call the sergeant to report the police accident.

Ever since then, the tank lid was brought up every time Barney saw him, and he had to admit it was worth it. Good friends are hard to find, and colleagues you can really trust even harder. Barney belonged to a different era of policing, before the advent of response times and ticky boxes, and key performance indicators. Barney was a real copper, even if Mick wasn't a real police driver.

Andy was still smiling at the thought of big Mick Habergham climbing out of his tank when the blue Ford Escort shot out of the side road in front of them.

*

Ham floored the accelerator and tightened his grip on the wheel.

"Whoah. He's shifting."

The Escort was already a hundred yards away and moving fast. He dropped into second gear and raced the engine to build up speed then slipped into third, his heart pounding. Andy was fidgeting with his seatbelt and Ham could sense his impatience at not being behind the wheel himself.

Sixty miles an hour through residential streets. They shot past the end of Pelham Terrace and for a moment it was as if they'd come full circle, ending the night as they'd begun, only this time there was no dog bite. The Escort was pulling away along the wide straight road and Ham flicked on the blue lights but ignored the siren. The driver knew they were following and the blue lights were just so he could be charged with failing to stop for a police officer.

Sixty-five miles an hour...

There was no other traffic on the road and it ran straight as an arrow to the outskirts. A parade of shops on the Bell Dean Estate flashed by.

Seventy...

The road was curving to the left now, running up the hill towards Highfield crossroads. Andy was shouting down the radio, giving their position and a description of the car. Blue Ford Escort five-door.

"Did you get the number?"

"No."

Ham was concentrating on keeping the patrol car steady. *Seventy-five...*

Even with his foot all the way to the floor the patrol car was flagging. They needed the traffic car on a straight run like this, the Volvo T5 or the Mondeo. Among the backstreets they might have a chance but they were never going to catch him on an open road. The Escort was growing smaller. Then it was gone. Vanished in the blink of an eye. Andy howled as if in pain.

"Shit. Where'd it go?"

Ham kept the speed up until they reached the last sighting then slowed down. A network of narrow streets ran off both sides of the road, through terraced houses and back-to-backs. Andy reported where they'd lost the car and the Dalek voice on the radio acknowledged.

"Shit."

If there was one thing got Andy's goat it was losing a car, closely followed by losing a chase on foot. In fact losing anyone he was after. Ham on the other hand was just glad he'd been wearing his seatbelt. He was certain that the alarm call with Barney would have gone differently if he'd had his seatbelt on. He just didn't feel comfortable without it, like an egg that wasn't in its eggcup. Once he hit any corners he felt as if he would roll right over. No, at least tonight he had belted up. He'd had enough of trees trying to grab him through the window.

The adrenalin slowly drained out of his body and he coasted round the side roads looking for a car with its engine running and doors open. Several lights were still on in the neighbouring houses but for the moment he didn't look through their windows. The worlds around him were safe from his prying eyes for now.

It soon became obvious the car had got away. The streets on the left were part of a small estate but the ones on the right lead onto a country lane that eventually ran into Alderton Village to the east. That in turn dropped back down the hill to the spread of houses from the council estate, the most likely destination for a stolen car. Tomorrow morning it would probably be found burnt-out in old man Townend's field and he would complain again about the lack of police action. There had been five cars dumped on his farm in the last month and it was scaring his sheep. Ham could sympathise with him. At least he didn't keep pigs. He was about to head back towards town in search for fresh windows when their call sign crackled over the radio.

"Where's Chagrin Avenue?" he asked.

"Back towards town, then left before you get there. Lower Grange."

"What can they find to argue about at this time of night?"

"At Lower Grange, anything."

Ham turned the car round and nodded. Lower Grange was the shit end of the council estate and they could disagree that sky was up. He pulled out onto the main road as the shift headed towards midnight and another ruined evening.

79 Chagrin Avenue

The party had gone well, Trevor thought, until he made the mistake of showing the wedding video. It wasn't the biggest mistake of his life, marrying his first wife, Joyce, topped that list, but inviting her to the family party along with his current wife, Shirley, came a close second. Playing the tape of his first wedding in the presence of his second wife was a photo finish and could easily pass both if things didn't improve tonight. He wouldn't have shown it at all if he hadn't been drinking but in order to survive an evening with his family, drinking to excess was a necessity not an option.

He went into the kitchen to avoid the fallout but the council house walls couldn't hide the noise and he wondered once again why he hadn't bought something better with the money? Money and family. Too much of the first and the second came out of the woodwork. If blood was thicker than water then Trevor Garner was thicker than both. He should have realised that paying for a party then inviting the family round was a recipe for disaster. His stepsons hated each other only slightly less than they hated him, and having them under the same roof put an almighty strain on a marriage built on a bed of sand.

Rebound effect. That was the problem. His marriage to Joyce had outlasted his teeth, only two of which remained, but not his drinking and when the accident took away his liveli-hood the drinking got worse. The marriage fell apart but he couldn't live without a woman in his life so he'd quickly married Shirley without thinking too hard about it. Thinking wasn't his strong suit and the repercussions were huge and immediate. The stepsons from hell. Rebound. Bounced out of the frying pan into the fire.

That was five years ago and the ex-boxer expected things to get better with time, but time was against him as well. It shafted him more firmly than his brother, then waited with an ace up its sleeve to stick it to him once more. Money. It wasn't the root of all evil but his family's love of it was.

Shirley screamed at her children in the living room and the kids yelled back. There was a thump against the wall followed by a rush of bodies. Joyce was crying so loud that she almost drowned out the commotion. Henry's voice rose above the noise, a calming influence amid the chaos. Henry Blake was a friend of the family and probably the only sane person there, but he was fighting a losing battle in this game of family fortunes.

More screaming, then the door opened and Wayne was shoved into the kitchen. The fifteen year-old's face was tear-stained and red but more importantly he was pissed. Smashed out of his tiny skull. Trevor fingered a sausage roll on the table, looking at the spread Shirley had put on with something approaching awe. There were plates of little triangular sandwiches with the crusts cut off, bowls of pickles and crisps, and a selection of quiches, pork pies and sausage rolls. A cakestand rose in the middle with cherry Bakewells, chocolate rolls and sponge cakes. It was a feast fit for kings. Instead it got the Garners.

Wayne stalked to the back door and sulked. Outside, Wesley barked and jumped at the handle, assuming that the shadow through the glass was there to let him in. The dog was banished from the party, chained in the back garden until the festivities ended. The dog didn't know how lucky it was. Trevor spied something on the table and picked up a vol-au-vent.

"Hair of the dog."

He held the savoury out to Wayne. A wiry dog hair stuck

out of the filling like a feather in a cap. Trevor laughed at his own joke proving he was pissed as well. Wayne not only didn't find it funny but couldn't see the hair anyway.

"Fuck off."

The shouting carried on in the front room and Marty's voice spiralled above Shirley's. The front door slammed.

"What have you and your brother fallen out over now?"

"Mind yer own fuckin' business. You're not my dad."

"I know, but he is your brother. You could at least try and get on. For your mother's sake."

"That why you put the video on? For mum's sake?"

Despite being three sheets to the wind the teenager had boxed Trevor into a corner with just one question. The broken nose and spread ears showed that he had been a battler in his youth, fast and nimble with a left that could send you into next Wednesday. What went on between his ears was a different matter. His business acumen was passable but thinking on his feet wasn't even close.

"Come on. I didn't mean any harm."

Wayne glowered across the mountain of sandwiches and said nothing. Trevor plucked the hair off the vol-au-vent and put it back on the plate. The noise in the living room was turning down but Wesley still barked in the back garden. Trevor wished he'd set up a bar in here because he really needed a drink now. Wayne had the same thought and moved towards the door.

"Drink."

Despite agreeing in principle Trevor blocked his way.

"Not yet. Let things calm down a bit first."

The teenager looked as if he was going to argue, bracing his shoulders for a lunge at the door, then a dull-eyed look seeped into his eyes, taking the starch out of his pose. Seeing the shoulders hunch down, Trevor brought his fists up, planting his feet for a solid base, and that's when the door opened behind him.

"Aw leave him alone."

41

Susie pushed under Trevor's arm.

"You're always picking on him."

Wayne's girlfriend pressed her ample breasts into his stomach, holding him tight.

"I wasn't—" was all Trevor got out before Shirley screamed in his ear.

"Leave my boy alone, Trev. He's just depressed."

"HE'S depressed? Fuck me."

"It's not Trevor's fault."

Joyce stuck to the first wife's prerogative of poking her nose in whenever she could. It had the desired effect and Shirley went ballistic.

"Who invited you anyway? Get out of my fuckin house."

"Make me, bitch."

The women squared up to each other, looking like a pair of wobbly bookends. Neither of them had worn well, carrying more folds of flesh than Hannibal the Cannibal. Whoever said that men grow distinguished with age while women just grow old was absolutely right. These two had never been bathing beauties even in their youth.

Auntie Alice sat on the settee nonplussed. The oldest person in the room, she had lost her sense of hearing long before she lost her teeth, and the crimped lips and collapsed mouth proved she'd lost them years ago. The ones she'd been wearing tonight didn't fit, so she'd taken them out and couldn't find them. The sight of Shirley and Joyce squaring up was the first she knew of any trouble. Trouble gave her wind, and at the first sign of it she farted long and hard.

Henry stood between the bookends beginning to wish he'd never started the business with Trevor, or moved next door to the neighbours from hell. His plans for a carefree retirement were constantly thwarted by the explosive domestic disputes. With patience that suggested a second career in the diplomatic corps he separated the combatants.

"Ladies, ladies."

Neither woman was in the mood for acting like a lady and Shirley stabbed a finger past him at her husband's former wife.

"You keep yer bloody eyes off my husband."

Henry tried to block any further contact.

"It's not me it's him."

"Bitch."

Henry waved his arms up and down slowly as if directing a Jumbo jet into its hangar. The movement calmed him more than the women, reminding him of those funny oriental exercises he'd seen on Channel Four. The women were about to get serious when Wayne diverted their attention.

"Gone to smash my fuckin' flat hasn't he?"

Trevor stood aside, exasperated.

"He was only kidding, love," Shirley said.

She forgot about Joyce and walked round the settee towards the kitchen.

"You know what he's like."

"Wouldn't happen if you two tried to get on."

Trevor returned to his favourite theme. Family harmony.

"He's gonna smash me flat up."

Susie pressed her breasts into him so hard they spread under his arms. The gesture went some way toward calming him. It also went some way to reminding him what the argument had been about in the first place and it wasn't anything to do with the wedding video.

"Fuckin' bastard. I'll kill him if he comes back."

"No, baby. Don't be silly," Susie said.

"Kill him."

Trevor went to the mini-bar in the living room. Things were spiralling out of control and he wondered why he'd married into this jungle. Aunt Alice farted again, the stress of the situation getting to her. While Trevor poured another Johnny Walker, Henry came up behind him.

"I feel like I should have brought my crash helmet."

"No. The crash happened years ago."

"Sorry. I didn't mean that crash."

"Me neither. Getting married again. That was the accident."

"You should never have given him the business."

They were silent for a moment. Trevor thought about the man who wasn't there, his brother Pat, surprised to find that most of the animosity had faded. The security firm he had built up with his brother was thriving, had been doing well when he gave it up, and it was the thread that held the family together and tore them apart. Garner Security International. The International had been added since the split, but they had been heading that way even then. Marty drove for the firm, when he could be bothered turning up, and Wayne considered Pat to be more of a stepfather than Trevor.

"Swings and roundabouts," Trevor said.

"See-saws more like."

Roller coasters mirrored Trevor's life more accurately, the only constant over the last few years being his friendship with Henry. They had started the security firm together back in their dim distant youth and had stuck together through thick and thin. Henry had argued against letting Pat be a partner in the first place, but for Trevor blood was thicker than water. Family was family. End of story.

Henry continued to do most of the thinking and much of the work while Trevor slid into drink, pressured by the constant drain of his brother and the guilt of letting him in. Henry was known as Hank around the factory, an affectionate term that was quickly bastardised by Pat. Hank the Wank he called him and not just behind his back. Henry was just too nice to argue about it and that made Trevor feel even guiltier, resulting in more drink.

The 'coup-de-tat' came six years ago. Henry worked as hard as ever but Trevor was becoming a liability. He was an alcoholic. The decisions he made were ill judged and the money he earned he pissed up the wall. Customers were turning their backs on the firm, embarrassed to be dealing with a drunk. Henry saw what was coming but was too polite to intervene.

Pat bought Trevor out for what amounted to peanuts.

Henry stayed with the firm but his influence evaporated until he finally took early retirement. Marty still worked there and Shirley had a soft spot for her husband's brother. Even Wayne was on Pat's side. Only Henry stood by Trevor and he would never forget it. Family was one thing, friendship a stronger bond altogether.

"Came out of a clear blue sky though didn't it?"

Trevor remembered the crash that almost killed him and the compensation that he received six months ago following a four-year legal battle. It actually came out of anything but a clear blue sky. Trevor's life hadn't been a clear blue sky since the boxing days of his youth. At least then you knew who was hitting you. These days you had to watch your bed in case you were nurturing a nest of vipers and if anything could bring out the snake in his family it was money. He had too much money now for any kind of happy home life.

"Get off him you little slut."

Shirley dragged at Susie's clothes but the busty blonde clung to Wayne like a limpet on a storm-tossed rock. Trevor downed his drink and prepared to intervene. Henry was too polite again to suggest that might be a bad idea. If he had spoken up then the entire evening might have been saved. As it was the call to the police was only minutes away.

Wayne mumbled something to his mother and Susie flung an arm out to dislodge Shirley's grip. Auntie Alice cringed in her seat and tried not to break wind. Trevor mustered as much calmness as he could and walked round the settee to the kitchen.

"No. It's Wayne I'm with," Susie said.

"Oh yeh. That's not what Marty said is it?" Shirley screamed.

"Gonna smash my flat."

Wayne slipped into a different conversation altogether.

Trevor's heart sank. He knew Marty was quite a lad about town, sleeping with half the office staff at Garner Security International. Somehow he managed to persuade the girls that

45

it was beneficial to their prospects, and since GSI's recruiting drive didn't climb much higher than the socially deprived they didn't know any better. He'd even been known to chat up the daughters of the security guards, a habit that Trevor thought was walking on thin ice. The guards were often no more than rent-a-thugs and you wouldn't want to get on the wrong side of any of them.

Now it sounded like Marty had crossed the boundary between good taste and family territory, something Susie Q would know nothing about. He suddenly felt sorry for his younger stepson. Nobody had asked where Marty had been when he slipped out earlier but Trevor would bet a pound to a pinch of shit it was a piece of skirt. The only thing in Marty's defence tonight was that Susie had been here all the time.

Trevor reached the kitchen and was about to pour oil on troubled waters when the front door slammed and Marty stormed in.

"What's that fuckin' dickhead saying now?"

Auntie Alice couldn't keep it in any longer. Henry's shoulders sagged. Joyce was just happy to see trouble that had nothing to do with her. It served Shirley right for stealing her husband.

"Bastard."

Wayne tried to disentangle himself from Susie's breasts. Trevor pointed at Marty.

"You. Wait outside."

"Or what?"

"Bastard," Wayne said.

"Quiet." To Wayne this time.

The whisky made Trevor's head swim but the headache came from his family as usual. Why did he invite them all round in the first place? Why couldn't he just enjoy the money by himself and leave this sea of torment?

When he entered the kitchen he knew why. The familiar yellow walls reflected the light like a Holy vision. The double-glazed windows were new but the kitchen units felt like they had been with him all his life. He'd built the mini-bar in the living room with his own hands, and the garden shed and greenhouse were both his handiwork. This shitty little cul-de-sac had been in his family for decades. Why should he leave it now just because he'd come into a bit of money? His blood began to boil.

"Shut up the pair of you."

Wayne pushed free of Susie, knocking her to one side. She overbalanced and Trevor reacted on instinct. He stuck his arms out and came up with a hot sweaty breast in each hand. Shirley screamed at him to let go but it was too late. Susie's momentum propelled them both into the table and even though Trevor released one tit to try and fend off the inevitable, the table took the brunt of their weight. It buckled, dropping plates of sandwiches and cakes onto the kitchen floor.

Marty cackled in the living room but Trevor might still have let it go if Wayne hadn't opened his mouth.

"Can't handle anything, you old bastard? Even took your brother to make you any money."

That was it. The red mist dropped over Trevor's eyes. His fists clenched as he came up off the floor, his mind snapping back to a cold autumn day on the way back from school. The surprise blow had knocked him to the ground but even as a child he was more dangerous when he was down. The boxer resurfaced in him like a kraken from the deep and he lunged at Wayne.

Shirley screamed again and Auntie Alice fainted. Henry was already calling the police before the first blow was struck.

*

It was amazing how often house numbers followed a pattern. This was the second seventy-nine of the night. Ham didn't have to look through the window to see into another world this time because that other world had spilled into the front garden. An over-excited dog almost ran under the wheels as Ham

47

slammed on the brakes, immediately calling for back-up. This was a war zone.

Midnight struck across the ruins of the family party and Sunday night slipped into Monday morning. The shift was only a quarter done but already Ham felt as if it would go on for-ever. He climbed out of the car and took stock before charg-ing in. That was something Barney had taught him, especially after the naked woman with the broken glass. That was a story Andy could do without for now. Maybe he'd tell him at the end of the shift.

But he wouldn't. Ham wouldn't be saying anything at all at the end of this shift.

A single orange streetlamp bathed the garden in a hellish glow, stark shadows darting about amid the cacophony of sound. A lad of about twenty shouted towards the house while two fat ladies stood in front of the open door. One shouted back at him then the other shouted at her. Their voices cut through Ham worse than Ricki Lake's, or fingernails on the blackboard. The dog ran back into the garden and circled them all, barking and yelping.

Ham tried to pinpoint the main threat. Judging by the ver-bal abuse and his posture that had to be the youth in the gar-den. Ignoring the gate, Ham stepped over the low wooden fence. Andy followed. The young lad turned towards them and braced himself but said nothing. That should have cut the noise by half but one of the women dashed over, screeching at the top of her voice.

"Inside. He's inside. I think he's going to kill him."

There was more shouting from the house and Ham saw hurried figures through the window. Andy was already mov-ing and Ham was undecided which way to go. If there was trouble inside he couldn't let Andy deal with it alone but the lad out here still looked threatening. The lad made Ham's mind up for him.

"Who the fuck called you?"

Andy was almost at the door and that's the only thing that

saved the garden gobshite from being arrested there and then. Ham turned on him, sticking a firm jaw into his face.

"I don't know who started this. But if you say another word before I go in that house I know who'll be ending it. Button it and bugger off."

He didn't wait for a response, following Andy into the house. First priority, back up your partner. He snapped off a code six into the radio, letting control know they'd arrived. The two fat ladies parted like the Red Sea, all ripples and swells, and then followed him in.

As often happened the inside of the house bore little resemblance to the picture he'd seen through the window. The brightly coloured living room was just a two dimensional rendition from outside, like a cheap movie without any real depth or feeling. Inside it became a 3D thrill-fest together with Sensurround and Smellavision. It was the difference between the Hyde Park fleapit and the Odeon Leicester Square.

An old lady with no teeth lay on the settee and a smartly dressed pensioner was comforting a busty blonde near the mini bar. There was broken glass in the fireplace and a Phillips TV hissed static in front of the window. Smellavision kicked in with a mixture cooked pastry and marsh gas. Either there was egg mayonnaise on the menu or someone had farted. The shouting was coming from the kitchen. Andy stood between what looked like a father and son combination.

"Calm down. Calm down."

He pointed to the older man.

"You. Out there. Let me talk to you a minute."

Andy led the father into the living room, the youth swearing at his retreating back.

"Who smashed this glass?" Ham said to anyone who would listen.

"My son," one of the women said. "But it's all right. He's calmed down now."

The lad in the kitchen seemed anything but calm.

"My flat's fucked."

He slammed a fist against the worktop hard enough to rattle the pots.

Ham nodded toward Andy. *I'll talk to that one,* the look said. Without speaking they both knew what to do. Lift and separate. It worked for Playtex and it usually worked for uniform patrol in domestic situations. The first thing you learned was that feuding families can't talk straight while in sight of their opposite number. Some didn't talk straight anyway but at least you had a fighting chance if you kept them apart.

Ham noticed the sandwiches and cakes on the floor. Half the contents of the table had done a Mount Etna and erupted into the sea. Together with the broken glass in the fireplace this was further evidence of a disturbance. He made a mental note in case he needed it later. Sometimes when he attended domestic assaults the wife would make an initial complaint, only to withdraw it three days later. If the case was to be prosecuted they needed additional evidence. Signs of a disturbance and visible injuries could be important.

"Somebody didn't like the sandwiches."

Ham started lightly in the hope he might coax some information out of the youngster. It was a forlorn hope because the disgruntled pimple was in no mood to be coaxed.

"Who fuckin' cares?"

"Your mother might."

"Hmmph."

"Who've you been arguing with?"

"Mind yer own business."

Ham looked at the squashed cakes, anger colouring his cheeks. It was too early in the shift for this nonsense and definitely too late in the week to be locking up from a party. He stood in front of the teenager.

"Look, don't piss me about. We can deal with this nice and easy or as rough as you like. For now I feel like the easy approach. If nobody's making any claims of damage or assault we might be able to sort this out without anyone getting locked up. Do you want to be locked up? Because you're looking favourite at the moment."

The boy didn't answer, simply looking down at his feet. Ham took that as a no.

"Right. What's been going on?"

"Just a family argument."

"Do you live here?"

"No. I've got a flat. If it's still in one piece."

"What's that supposed to mean?"

"Nothing."

Ham felt the status quo was being maintained. Anyone that spoke to the police told part of the truth and part of a lie and what snippets of truth peppered the tale were like the tip of an iceberg. Nobody seemed to be injured and apart from a couple of broken glasses and a few sandwiches there was no damage to speak of.

"Wait here while I talk to your mum. And stay cool. Turn your collar up or something."

He went into the living room where Andy was talking to the father near the front window. The mother came straight over.

"Don't take him to the police station. Please. He's just had too much to drink."

"Did he break the glass?"

She nodded, fighting back the tears.

"His stepdad?" Ham nodded to the man who'd been arguing in the kitchen.

"Party was going fine until he'd had too much to drink."

"Who?"

"Wayne. My son. Can you take him home? He'll be all right in the morning."

"He said something about his flat."

"His brother stormed off, but I don't think he'd really smash Wayne's flat."

Another snippet of truth. Ham tested it against the other pieces. The lad shouting in the garden. The stepfather arguing with Wayne in the kitchen. The signs of disorder. And the drink. That was usually the bottom line. Beer in, brains out. If he had a pound for every calm and reasonable person he saw change into a raving beast after a few drinks he'd be a wealthy man.

"I don't think it would be a good idea him going home. Is there anywhere else he can stay tonight?"

"He can stay with me," the blonde girl said. "My mum won't mind."

"Where do you live?"

"Lady Lane."

"Other side of town? Up by the park?"

"Yes. I can ring to make sure it's okay."

Ham glanced over at Andy who nodded his approval. No complaints of assault. This could be the easy way out but in the back of his mind he felt it was going too smoothly. Domestics never went smoothly. He crossed his fingers. On the last night of the week you wanted anything but grief and it looked as if they might have sidestepped grief quite handily.

"Hang on."

Ham went back to Wayne who was being sick over the washing up.

"Wayne. Listen up."

The head came up but the neck didn't want to hold it.

"You can't stay here tonight…"

"Aw get fucked."

"…but your girlfriend says you can stay at her house."

"While me fuckin' flat gets trashed?"

A bit of oil was needed if Ham was going to smooth this over.

"We'll go check your flat. I'm on all night. We can pass it every half hour or so."

He meant it too, even though he'd have little chance if the night kept on like this.

"I can stay here."

"No you can't. There's been too much trouble tonight and we need to make sure it doesn't flare up again. That means keeping you and your stepdad apart."

"Her mum won't let me stay. Don't even like me."

"I wonder why?"

Wayne barfed up another dry heave, his stomach already empty.

"Don't splash the sandwiches. Somebody might still be hungry."

Ham thought this might work out all right but Wayne's brother niggled at the back of his mind. He wondered if he'd let the wrong person go, especially since the garden gobshite had given them such a colourful welcome.

"Wipe your mouth and let's get going."

Wayne dabbed at his mouth then followed Ham into the living room. Andy was waiting at the front door, apparently finished with the boxer. They almost made it outside when the hungry jaws of family snapped at his heals. Suddenly the mother saw her son being led away by the police and she snapped.

"Nnooo... Don't take him away."

"He'll be okay here," Wayne's stepfather said, ignoring the fact that they'd been at each other's throats when the cavalry arrived.

"Fuck," Wayne said, keeping up the standard of his conversation.

"Please, please."

His mother grabbed Ham's arm in her pudgy hands.

"He's not under arrest. We're taking him to her house."

Susie Q beamed as if she'd been chosen from the audience of *Who Wants To Be A Millionaire*? Ham tried to guide them both towards the front door but the mother wouldn't let go. Through the window blue lights flashed across the garden as the other units arrived. The sight of them sent the woman into a frenzy.

"Nnooo, nnooo, nnooo. Don't lock him away."

Ham nodded at Andy, then through the window.

"I'll tell them they can go."

Andy went outside and the lights stopped.

"We're not locking him away. We're taking him away so there'll be no more trouble tonight. He's not going to a cell. He's going to a fluffy pink bedroom where his girlfriend's mother can whip him if he tries anything."

Susie grinned. Looking at her Ham doubted if it would be Wayne doing the trying and looking at Wayne he doubted if she'd have any luck. The woman let go. She stood in the garden while Ham put the drunken youth and his girlfriend in the back of the patrol car. He glanced through the lighted window and wondered if the world beyond it would be less volatile now the lad had been removed but doubted it. In his experience ex-wives and current wives did not mix. Add alcohol and you had a time bomb waiting to go off.

Ham started the engine, Wayne said, "Fuck" one more time, confirming that both brothers were on the same level. *Well, we got away with that,* Ham thought as he reversed out of the cul-de-sac. They didn't get halfway to the girlfriend's house before he realised he was wrong.

*

"Why have I been arrested?" Wayne asked for the third time.

They were heading into town on a darkened road that was almost deserted. Ham kept his eyes on the road as he spoke but his mind was beginning to fray with the futility of his answers.

"I told you. You're not under arrest. We're taking you to Susie's mum's."

They were all on first name terms now, except for Wayne who had steadfastly refused to acknowledge his captors. Andy chipped in to help.

"Look, you can sleep it off at Susie's and sort it out tomorrow."

"No. You're fuckin' taking me away. Aven't done fuck all wrong."

"Shush love."

Susie held Wayne's hands in her lap. Ham looked in the mirror.

"Wayne. Think of us as a free taxi."

"Fuck off."

Wayne was getting more agitated, thumping his fists into the back of Ham's seat.

"You fucking bastards are taking me away. Go on then, fuckin' lock me up. You don't even care about my flat."

Ham gritted his teeth.

"I'll tell you what I care about. I care about keeping the peace, and at the moment you are not keeping the peace in this car. Now I'll tell you for the last time. You're going to Susie's, but if you swear at me again…"

Ham's temperament was being sorely tested and he didn't trust himself to continue. They were away from the family party and he just wanted to drop this idiot off before there was any more trouble. Over the years he'd been called every name under the sun and mostly he let it flow over him but there was a limit. Trying to help Wayne instead of arresting him then being abused for doing it was close to the limit. Wayne calmed down.

"All right. I'm sorry. I know you're only doing your job."

Then he snapped again.

"But fuck me, why fuckin' lock me up?"

Ham stopped the car and turned to face the teenager, his face red with anger.

"Look, Wayne. Last chance. One more word out of you before we get to Susie's and you're spending the night in a cell. Any word. Understand?"

Wayne opened his mouth but Ham raised a finger. Wayne didn't speak.

"Good."

The streetlamps threw orange pools along the main road, separated by expanses of darkness. Ham felt he was sliding into one of those pools as the night wore on. Midnight had slipped behind them and now it was a case of picking up the pieces. Angela popped into his mind and he wondered if the pieces there were too badly broken. Whatever else he had to deal with tonight there was a decision to be made.

"Yeh but…" Wayne said.

"Not a word."

"Fuckin' ace."

Wayne's face contorted with rage. Ham saw it and knew they'd lost the battle.

"Fuckin' ace. You bastards don't know what I mean. My own fuckin' brother."

"That's it."

Ham spun the car round in the middle of the road.

"You *are* under arrest now. Tell the cell walls how bad you've been treated because I don't care any more."

He glanced at Susie who shrugged her shoulders. *I tried*, her expression said.

"And if you thump that seat again I'll slap you with resisting arrest."

Monday: 00.50 hrs

"I think me and Angela are going to split up," Ham said.
They were parked in a tree-lined lane overlooking Quarry View
Cottage, a lavishly extended detached that was barely a cottage and didn't have a view of the quarry at all. From where
they sat, in the shadows of a weeping willow tree, the view
was of a beautifully kept living room through full-length patio
doors. The patrol car's engine was silent and the lights turned
off.

It was the sight of the tidy living room that turned Ham's
thoughts towards Angela, whose domestic habits were anything but tidy. He could clean the kitchen as often as he liked
but she only had to walk in to turn it into a bombsite. She
managed to cover every flat surface with the contents of her
handbag and, as much as he loved her, seventeen years of
wading through shit was getting him down. That and other
things.

Andy didn't know what to say. The show through the window was due to start at any moment and the curve ball caught
him by surprise. He looked at his partner to see if he was
starting one of his jokes but Ham's face was a charcoal sketch
in the dark interior. He thought there was a glimmer of white
in Ham's eyes but that could have been the reflection of the
patio light.

Ham sighed as if the statement had drained his energy. In
a way it had because the effort of finally acknowledging his

fears was enormous. He'd been with Angela seventeen years, seven of those in the town house they owned, and he married her two years ago. There wasn't a day went by when he didn't regret it. Things hadn't been running smoothly even before that so why the hell get married? But he knew why. A noble cause in a harsh world.

As he waited for Lady Godiva to enter the perfect world beyond the patio doors, Ham's mind turned to the one aspect of his life with Angela that *was* perfect. Sex. He felt like a stallion riding the range, a ghost rider in the sky who was always in the saddle until way past midnight. He knew she felt the same and if her explosive orgasms were anything to go by she felt it a damn sight more than he did.

He hadn't always felt like that. As a teenager he was too shy to even ask a girl out, let alone contemplate carnal knowledge. Ham spent countless hours outside the Odeon waiting for his dates to turn up. He missed the beginning of dozens of films because he waited until the last minute before realising that he'd been stood up again. Being embarrassed wasn't the worst thing at the time. There were two things that were sacrilege to the young Michael Habergham, someone telling him how a film ended before he saw it and missing the first five minutes. The director didn't spend millions setting the scene for his audience to miss the vital clues in the opening frames.

Compared to that, being stood up a few times paled into insignificance. Except it didn't. Those crushing blows hurt deeper than he cared to admit. He had once gone on a date so full of enthusiasm that his parents cringed; praying that this time it would be different. An hour later they were sitting in front of the *Morecambe and Wise Show* when the front door slammed and Ham's footsteps stormed to his bedroom, the pain settling in their hearts as well as his.

In the army he had crawled to first base a time or two, with the help of plenty of Bacardi and Coke, but he still wasn't the sexual swordsman he hoped to be. No stallions in his herd just yet. Weekend leave saw him head for the capital, searching

London's backstreets for those illicit doorbell messages, "French Model" or "Private Massage" that promised so much. They usually didn't live up to expectation, either a fat hairy bacon-slicer or a non-English speaking European with an old granny collecting money before you entered.

One woman had been particularly nice. Francine. She was an attractive forty-year-old living in her own flat near Paul Raymond's Revue Bar. The red neon sign flashed through her window when the bar was open, lending the tiny bedroom a romantic air it didn't deserve. She sensed his inexperience when she asked him to undress and wash first. He stood bare-arsed in front of the sink and washed his hands. Stifling a laugh that would have been disastrous she stood beside him, warming her hands with soap and water, and washed his member until it was erect. It was the most exciting sexual experience of his life to date.

They became good friends, or as good as their situation allowed, and for two years he was a regular customer. The alley opposite the revue bar grew familiar and whenever he had weekend leave he would visit. It was a shock when he called one winter's evening only to find the label in the bell push changed. A stranger offered him sex for five pounds and it was all he could do to fight back the tears as he turned her down. Francine was no more.

Still, he was on the sexual map, but a long way from stallionship. Getting sex from someone who was expected to supply it was one thing. Trying to get it from a casual acquaintance was something else. He didn't drink but found alcohol necessary in order to bolster his resolve. Coca-Cola was his poison so adding Bacardi became his road to self-confidence.

At military dances a few Bacardi and Cokes put him on the right track but he still found himself approaching dogs instead of babes because he reckoned there was less chance of a refusal. Chatting up some of the women from the Royal Corps of Transport needed a few drinks first. Driving ten-ton lorries did nothing for their looks and plenty for their forearms. They were fearsome propositions and, as he found out, less interested in him than each other.

The Indonesian au-pair girl from behind the camp was a step in the right direction. She was fascinated with his uniform and more than willing to share a bit of flesh when they babysat her employer's children. She tasted of sweet-and-sour pork and wore a constant sheen of sweat that forced him to hang on when they kissed in case he slipped off. What bothered him was the fact that she wouldn't go all the way in the house, displaying a sense of loyalty that meant she could strip down her undies with gay abandon but sex was definitely not on the cards.

Not until they went to the pictures that was. After watching Clint Eastwood paint the town red in *High Plains Drifter* he walked Sheng Lee through the camp, keeping to the warm darkness of the rugby fields. On a grassy bank between pitches they settled down to some heavy petting and it wasn't long before they were down to their underwear. When she released his prong he mounted her with all the enthusiasm of Black Beauty. Unfortunately, in the dark, he'd taken her knickers off but forgotten about the tights. It was like making love to a trampoline, bouncing in and out until his erection disappeared.

It wasn't until years later that he realised you could manipulate yourself into a woman without shame. In all those James Bond films he'd watched, the coupling just seemed to happen naturally. Several porn nights on camp taught him that a little teasing and parting of the lips worked wonders. Hell, half the fellas in those films spent all their time playing with themselves whenever they weren't in somebody's mouth or better. The knowledge moved him up the ladder towards becoming a sexual paragon.

With Angela that reached its peak, but not at first. In the early days of their courtship sex had proved something of a disaster. His anxiety about pleasing her meant he didn't have the tools to please her at all and after several months of foreplay his weapon proved to be anything but lethal. It had been spiked by his own nerves. He didn't feel nervous at the time, his attention to foreplay proving effective as she became unhinged in his company, but obviously somewhere in the back of his mind the pressure of having to perform held him back.

He didn't realise back then but Angela's shyness was taking a dent as well. She thought it was her fault and his lack of thrust made her feel even worse. In their own minds each blamed themselves. He suggested they should buy a set of splints then at least he could double it over and put it in sideways. The attempt at humour helped but didn't solve the problem. In the end it was love that unlocked the door to their passion.

After six months of fumbling they felt comfortable enough that the stallion slipped its reins and rode free. Love and sex became two hands washing each other. Years later, when they talked about those embarrassing times, Angela admitted it was his delayed delivery that made her feel so safe with him. Sex for Ham was more than a one-night stand; it had to come from a loving relationship. Ham reckoned she felt secure because she knew he couldn't have a one-night stand, an erection wouldn't come until he'd been dating for six months.

That was the up side. The down side of living with Angela hit him straight away, he just didn't recognise it at first. Love and sex coloured his world with rose tinted glasses. Standing on broken nutshells in his bare feet woke him up.

The kitchen was the first place he began to notice how untidy she was. Every part of it, not just the worktops, or the dining room, or the sink. Every flat surface became a storage facility for Angela's stuff. And by stuff he meant everything. Cigarette packets, make-up, newspapers, torn envelopes, dirty cups, and decaying food. It began to irritate him that he could never make her a cup of tea without having to wash her cup first.

"You are allowed to wash up now and again."

"Thanks. That's very kind of you."

He couldn't stay mad at her long. He loved her too much.

The other drawback to getting angry was that whenever he did, she burst out laughing. His stream of invective was so colourful that she found him amusing. He never came straight out and told her to do something; he always slipped into it sideways. One morning when he got up, the kitchen was its usual bombsite. She sat with her feet up on the worktop in front of the TV, blissfully unfazed. When he found her cup he waved it in her face.

"Oh look. The pixies have forgotten one. I'm sure you think they come out at night and wash the pots, because you never do it yourself."

"I think I'll leave the ironing out tonight. See if they'll do that as well."

He couldn't help laughing and that always broke the spell. No matter how angry it made him she could always diffuse the situation with a smile. If that failed, all she had to do was stroke his cock and he was powerless. How can you argue with that?

The peanuts ushered a change in the balance of power; Angela's power to sweep his arguments under the carpet, or not sweep them under the carpet in the case of the nutshells. They'd been living together for two years and some of the shine had gone from their home life. Little things that had merely been irritants early on developed more bulk with the passage of time. Sex was still great, just less frequent, and when she put her mind to it she could still twist him round her little finger; tease him with all her fingers to be exact. It was his desire that began to wane and the reason for that was almost everything she did and said. Mostly what she didn't do.

One morning he padded barefoot round the kitchen making Angela's cup of tea. When he reached over the breakfast bar to hand her the cup, pain shot through his foot.

"What the bloody hell!"

He looked at the floor with undisguised annoyance. A Safeways carrier bag lay open next to the washing machine and half a dozen peanuts had spilled out. Some of the shells were empty, jagged teeth waiting for unwary feet. He picked up the bag as if it had a bad smell. Angela drank her tea, feet up, watching GMTV. An insipid presenter discussed the latest *Big Brother* eviction.

"What's this?" he asked.

"Peanuts for the squirrels."

Angela had recently taken to feeding the squirrels when she walked to work. They had become so used to her that she only had to rattle the bag and entire families of them came out of the trees.

"Well, there's no squirrels living in the washing machine."

He dropped the bag in the bin and started pulling pieces of broken shell out of his foot. In fairness they hadn't broken the skin but at the time shock lent them extra power. Pain, no matter how slight, was still pain in Ham's book.

"Don't throw them away."

"I'll throw more than them away if you don't start keeping this place tidy."

He glared at the spread of cosmetics on the worktop.

"And that's another thing. You only put foundation and lip-stick on. How come there's always two ton of make-up on here when you've gone to work?"

"Eyeliner."

"What?"

"Eyeliner as well."

"Well, even with eyeliner you don't add up to Mary Quant. Try binning what you don't use. Christ, you trowel it on and scrape it off anyway. You remind me of my dad with the but-ter."

He felt an urge to sweep the worktop clean but resisted. In years to come his anger would prove too strong and he would smash the bottles against the wall then feel guilty about it.

Standing on those nutshells opened his eyes. The irritants became niggles, and the niggles became eyesores that he wasn't prepared to put up with. A life of tidy wedded bliss seemed as far away as ever and things were going to get a lot worse. Forget the lids that never got closed, or the cigarette butts left standing all over the house like toy soldiers, or even the burn holes in the carpet when she nodded off with a cigarette in her hand. When she started coming home late, sometimes not coming home at all, the alarm bells began to ring.

Sitting in the patrol car beneath the weeping willow he felt like weeping himself. The enormity of his problems was too much to bear and now he'd broached the subject he found them too much to talk about. Thankfully Andy didn't press him. It was a blessing and a curse. Ham's problems were so bad that he needed to get them out of his system but they were so embarrassing that there was no one he could confide in. He'd always been able to talk to his mother, and his father too since he retired, but not about this. This was too personal.

"She's here," Andy said.

"Bang on time."

Ham glanced at his watch. They settled down in their seats in case she could see them, certain that she knew they were there anyway, and watched the show.

*

Ham watched with less eagerness than usual. Of all the windows he looked through during a nightshift this was the most perplexing. On the one hand watching a beautiful woman who liked to perform her nightly rituals in front of a plate glass window was pleasantly diverting; on the other, it turned him into the peeping Tom he didn't believe he was.

Andy had no such qualms. He practically drooled at the prospect of another strip show. It amazed Ham that they had managed to keep the weekend show a secret because if there was one thing he'd learned over the past twenty-six years it was that once the police got a whiff of a good thing they could strip it to the bone faster than a shoal of piranha.

Tat's fisheries knew by bitter experience what a mistake it

was to let the local footbeat officer have discount on fish and chips. Within six weeks the building was encircled by bobbies queuing out of the back door every teatime. By the time old man Tat finished discounting their meal breaks he was almost bankrupt. Eventually he called a halt and hoards of disgruntled police officers descended on the Chinese take-away further up the road. Mr Hing never forgave him, cursing him in some ancient dialect. When Mr Tat tripped over a box of prawn crackers and fell down the cellar steps he laid the blame squarely on the Chief Constable for letting his officers plague him in the first place, forgetting that he had opened the flood-gates himself by offering that illusive police discount.

The window at Quarry View Cottage remained their secret. Even Andy, who was notoriously loose-tongued, had kept it to himself. It had often been said that if you wanted to spread the word you should tell Andy in confidence. The fact that he'd slept with half the female members of the shift helped the flow of information.

Ham's reluctance to come here went deeper than that. He was in a privileged position, patrolling the streets through the night when most people were asleep in their beds. The early hours of the morning were a deeply satisfying time of day and he'd often park up and patrol on foot for a while soaking up the silence that only night could bring. During the day there were dozens of distracting noises – the rumble of traffic, or the lilting strains of far off music, or voices raised in conversation across a garden fence. Dogs barked and cats meowed and birds squawked their way through the daylight hours but once the sun went down and the night wore on they all faded to silence. Only the occasional car or overnight delivery truck broke the silence.

The quiet bred a calmness in Ham and once you bridged the hump of midnight – a time when even the quietest nightshift could be ruined – the clock wound down and only the windows remained. Drifting through the streets at patrol speed – something Andy didn't recognise because when he was behind the wheel there was only fast or faster – Ham could partake of his nightly passion, looking at the lives of his customers through the plate glass portal.

He was their guardian and that gave him the honour of overseeing their lives while they slept. Modern life being what it was there were many times when they didn't sleep; when they played out their one act plays on the set of their living rooms, or kitchens, or even the inner sanctum of their bedrooms. Mostly these were innocent domestic scenes, kitchen sink dramas, and he was moved once again by how many lives he would never touch. Sometimes they were more exciting, and the lady at Quarry View Cottage fitted into that category. It was Andy's favourite stop of the week.

For Ham it felt like a breach of trust, even though she obviously thrived on the performance. You don't get undressed in front of a full-length patio door with the lights on if you're worried about being seen and you don't take your time unless you're hoping someone's out there.

The woman was tall and slim with a perfect tan and blonde hair that hung around her shoulders. She wore a tight white halter neck top and khaki combat pants. Her slender fingers loosened the neck then grasped the bottom, pealing it over her head. Quivering brown flesh filled the bra and she continued to stare out of the window as she fingered the top of her trousers. She undid the button then paused, leaving the zip up for a moment.

"That's not her husband," Andy said.

A man had entered the room through the hall door and was standing beside the bookcase while she swayed gently in front of the window. She didn't appear to have noticed him.

"I didn't think he worked Sunday nights."

Ham scoured the driveway to see if his car was still there. It wasn't. They'd been coming here long enough to know that the woman parked her silver Ford Ka in the garage and her husband left his Rover in the drive. They didn't know what he did for a living but realised that he worked the occasional night, probably stocktaking, or completing some important business deal. He rarely did that on a Sunday night.

"Shit," Andy said.

The intruder was edging around the wall towards her as she unzipped the trousers. Her hips swayed as if in time to some hidden music. Ham grasped the door handle, ready to charge across the lawn if the man got any closer. The cottage was alarmed but it wouldn't be set until she went to bed. It was always the last thing she did after her nightly performance.

Sweat began to bead on Ham's lip; only it was nothing to do with the heat of the night or the restricting bulk of the stab vest. His first thought was, *how can we call this in when we're not supposed to be here anyway?* but he quickly banished that. One thing Barney had taught him was that you could make anything read right later; first you've got to do the right thing. Covering his back had become second nature ever since the tank lid incident.

The stranger was right behind her now. Ham opened the car door and put one leg out, bracing himself for the charge. Andy did the same. The woman slid her trousers down, revealing an inviting V of silky thong. As she stepped out of the trousers the man moved forward and...

Ham let out a sigh of relief that was tinged with shock. Andy slumped in his seat. Both closed their doors as quietly as they could. The woman spun to face the man, threw her arms around his neck, and as they began to kiss the first seeds of embarrassment crept into Ham's mind.

Quarry View Cottage

Shame mingled with the kiss and, as exciting as the contact was, Loren Elkins couldn't help thinking about her husband, Peter. Electricity sparked her flesh into a sea of goose bumps and the guilt added flavour to an already tasty dish. In the otherwise spotless living room she was about to besmirch her marriage with a completely unnecessary act of carnal desire.

Unnecessary because she was already being moderately satisfied by the husband who had left her for work tonight, but required by the age old credo of an-eye-for-an-eye. She sensed the dark presence outside in the lane and her excitement grew. The soft downy hairs on her stomach flared like a cornfield in the wind and her nipples hardened. Shame held her back though.

Loren Elkins was twenty-five, four years younger than her husband, but the gulf was much wider than could be counted in years. Even going back to their courtship – an outdated term for the monstrous couplings that had dotted their early years – she had realised that there were more differences than similarities between them.

Peter was fastidiously clean and tidy, while she was merely clean. Here was a man who ironed his handkerchiefs and kept his socks neatly folded in pairs at all times. It surprised her that he didn't wash them two at a time so they didn't get mixed up. He put the lid on anything that was left open, closed every door, and turned every light off if they were out of the room for thirty seconds.

The thing that amused her more than anything was his attitude to the rubbish. Their kitchen waste bin must be the tidiest in Christendom. He always put a fresh bin-liner in when it was emptied, and tore up old newspapers to line the bottom. When a new box of Fruit and Fibre was opened he would tear the box into quarters so it lay flat in the bin then squeeze the plastic inner into a long strip and tie it in a knot before putting that in as well. He argued that if you just screwed it up, the damn thing bloomed like a desert rose, taking up all the space.

He was a good provider though; giving her a steady home life she hadn't enjoyed since her parents' divorce. The shock of losing the cocoon of safety so early in life – she was only eight – forced her to withdraw into her shell, and it was only the advent of her teenage years that cleared the way for the exhibitionist she would later become. That exhibitionist blossomed in the safe surroundings of Quarry View Cottage. It came as quite a shock to Peter, who thought he'd married a demure girl who preferred to make love with the lights off.

"But the grass isn't cut," he said when she first suggested having sex on the lawn. It was a pleasant summer's evening and barbecues down the street filled the air with the smell of char-grilled chicken and sausage. The lawn in question was behind the cottage, sheltered from prying eyes by the garage and a battalion of conifers.

She laughed, an image of Peter doing it doggy fashion with three blades of grass stuck out of his backside like the daffodil in Carry On Nurse. She thought it was the likelihood of ruining the lawn that bothered him more than being seen. Loren could be very persuasive, and he wasn't exactly a prude himself, but he took some persuading the first time.

The child psychologists who took her out of school after some of her more outrageous exploits said she was seeking revenge but they could never explain who she was seeking revenge against. Doing gym class without a bra was one thing but forgetting her knickers proved too much for the private school that her parents sent her to. It wasn't a residential school

70

but no matter how much they paid for her education she still came back to a broken home, living with her father and elder brother. Being in a house with no female company was the worst thing the courts could have allowed but by that time her mother was in no fit state to look after anyone. Liver failure was inevitable, the amount of alcohol she soaked up.

Marrying Peter was the first step to rebuilding her life, wiping the slate clean and starting afresh. Only some stains ran too deep to be wiped clean, they needed scrubbing and steaming and blasting away. Setting up home in this safe haven near the quarry should have gone a long way towards doing that, and she was happy with him. It was her lapses of etiquette that sometimes disturbed him, as exciting as they were, and not wanting grass up his arse was just part of it.

He knew that she undressed in front of the window. The sight had aroused him at first, when she used to do it in the bedroom. Lace curtains were fine during the day but after dark, with the lights on, she might as well be standing outside. That was his initial argument, but when he realised that that was what excited her he cut her some slack. After all, your wife getting excited in the bedroom had very definite benefits.

Then she had widened her field of operations, walking naked in the kitchen and the study, before settling on the double wide patio doors of the living room. Like all the other rooms in the house it was spotless, everything in its place. The shelves had just the right balance of books and ornaments, and the paintings on the walls were evenly spaced. Heavy-duty throw cushions created the impression of organised chaos when in fact they were strategically placed to blend with the deep-pile carpet and the Chinese rug.

They even made love on the settee several times after her nightly performances, but not until the curtains were drawn. A man who irons his handkerchiefs isn't going to be caught by the neighbours no matter how sexy his wife is. She was happy with that, accepting that his urges were less instinctive than hers.

Then he'd started working late.

The ghosts of her dysfunctional family came back to haunt her, stripping away any semblance of confidence she might have had. Her father's transgressions were being paid back on the daughter. Only they weren't. And now there was John Coniglio. Her mind raced as her body flowed into his arms and she didn't notice the car pull up in the driveway.

*

Ham watched with a mixture of excitement and guilt as the woman embraced her lover. He knew it must be her lover because her husband was a short overweight businessman and his car wasn't in the drive. He felt sorry for her. She didn't look like someone who would betray her husband and it seemed ironic that living in the kind of tidy house that Ham would die for she could be guilty of behaviour that he dreaded.

When the wheel began to come off his home life, deceitful behaviour was the first thing to rear its ugly head. The lies and the late nights, and eventually the nights when she didn't come home at all. In all the time he'd been with Angela he had never slept with anyone else. Sex with her was so good that he couldn't see the point. Why look for hamburger when you've got steak at home, as Paul Newman once said. To the best of his knowledge he'd never lied to her either, and it was the lies that tore him apart. The truth behind those lies came later, and were just as crushing.

Watching the illicit embrace simply proved a point. Lies destroy; going behind your partner's back destroys totally. He wanted to drive away but Andy's tongue was out. If he set off too fast he thought he'd cut his young partner's tongue off. Despite the emotional turmoil he kept his eyes on the slender bridge of bra stretched across the woman's back. Grubby brown hands reached for the clasp.

Andy was drooling, his mouth open in an idiot's gape.

Neither heard the car until its headlights swept the lane.

The silver Rover slid quietly past them and then reversed into the drive. The lights went off. Glancing back through the window Ham could see that the woman hadn't seen it either, then her husband got out carrying a stack of files.

*

Loren opened her eyes as the bra snapped open. John Coniglio slipped the smooth fabric off her shoulders and she felt his tight skin brush her nipples. The couple turned in a slow dance of love. She stared at her reflection in the window, picked out by discreet cavity lights in the ceiling. The lighting was more discreet than she was and looking at John's broad shoulders dwarfing her own slender frame she accepted that it wasn't a dance of love at all, but a dance of lust. Not even that really, it was musical revenge.

She remembered meeting him when he fitted the new bathroom suite. Peter had insisted that the towels were neatly folded two by two like animals queuing for the arc. He always insisted on things being in pairs. If he waited for a bus he'd have demanded two at a time. He was quite happy with the slime green bathroom suite they already had but the colour reminded Loren of puke. The sickly green stuff that Linda Blair had thrown up just before her head spun round in *The Exorcist*.

Plus she was tired of sitting in a bath where she could never get her knees wet without kneeling down. The bath must have been made for pygmies. It was so short that you could forget about lying down, you just had to sort of scrunch up to get your torso wet. The shower curtain annoyed her as well. Considering the cottage had been fully modernised the bathroom belonged in a bygone era of gaslights and fog-bound streets.

No. An up-to-date corner bath with separate shower cubicle was called for, and Peter being the dutiful husband – despite folding everything in pairs – had acceded to her wishes. A firm came round to survey the bathroom and that's when she met John Coniglio. It was bad timing because that was also when she began to suspect Peter was seeing someone else.

Standing half-naked in his arms she wondered again about his name. As she'd plucked up courage to invite him round the name had contorted in her mind, Johan Cunnilingus being her favourite. That surname fed her fantasy and as she became more certain that Peter was being unfaithful that was the act she wanted to use for revenge. In front of the window too. No point doing things by halves.

Coniglio hadn't taken much persuading. The bathroom was almost finished but this was the first time he was going to check her plumbing. With the moment almost upon her, she began to have second thoughts. Peter's face swam before her in the window, a ghostly vision carrying an armful of files. The vision drifted left and disappeared down the drive, too busy looking for his keys to see through the window.

Two by two, she thought. *Everything folded two by two.* She remembered him being annoyed that his secretary had filed the outgoing memos separately from the replies. The system was an affront to his orderly nature. He had started waiting until she left before redoing the filing cabinet, causing him to be late twice a week for the last three months.

Two by two.

The thought froze in her mind. Only last night he had told her that he'd finally got rid of the secretary. Not fired her – Peter couldn't turn the poor girl out on the street – but simply moved her sideways into storage accounts. From what he'd seen of the storage facility she should be perfectly at home there, the store-man thought a pair was the next hand down from a flush, his card-schools being legendary among middle-management.

Loren began to think she might have overreacted, another family trait handed down from her mother, and guilt flooded over her. She saw her naked flesh being pawed by the plumber and suddenly felt shy. For the first time since they'd moved into the cottage she felt like closing the curtains.

Then she heard the keys in the front door.

"Oh no."

She pushed John away. Panic froze her like a rabbit in the headlights of an oncoming car. She couldn't move. The cunnilingus man had no such problems. The trouble was that the front door led into the hallway, and the only other way out was through the kitchen where he'd come in. That was across the hall.

In her panic Loren began to hallucinate. Bright lights exploded in her head and a banshee wail rose and fell outside. She put her hands over her ears but the sound squeezed through them. Closing her eyes didn't keep the lights at bay either, the blue flashes penetrating her eyelids. John turned to look out of the window and she realised he could see them as well.

Suddenly the prospect of being abducted by aliens seemed a very real alternative to being caught by her husband. She'd seen *Close Encounters of the Third Kind*, when those funny lights flashed across the night sky but didn't think the aliens could suck her through the patio doors as long as she kept them locked. Being caught by her husband was definitely on the cards though.

John Cunnilingus didn't intend to get caught. The blue flashing lights outside were just the distraction he needed. While the keys stopped rattling in the front door he darted across the hall and out through the kitchen. Loren quickly pulled her top over her head and threw the bra and combat trousers onto the settee.

The police car screeched out of the lane with a squeal of tyres, blue lights and siren blaring. She didn't think she'd ever been happier to see the boys in blue. Peter came into the lounge carrying the files he'd brought home to fold up two by two, and her heart wept.

"I told you not to park too close to the road."

He noticed her thong showing beneath the white body top and put the files down.

"And I've told you about undressing with the curtains open."

For once she agreed, and closed them before folding into his arms, two by two.

Monday: 01.25 hrs

Ham was thankful for the panic alarm because it kept his mind away from Angela. The incident at Quarry View Cottage left him feeling depressed, and that wasn't a normal state of affairs for Mick Habergham. He was universally upbeat, with a smile and a glib remark for everyone he met. Even people he was arresting, most of the time.

The blue lights and siren did the trick, delaying the husband's entrance long enough to prevent another domestic. As a police officer, one of Ham's duties was to prevent and detect crime – it said so on the reverse of his warrant card; protect life and property, prevent and detect crime, and arrest offenders – so doing the blue-light-shuffle had fulfilled his responsibilities, preventing an argument that could well have turned nasty. He didn't know the couple but from past experience cheated husbands or wives often saw red, beating the living crap out of each other. Similarities to his own situation were too harsh to contemplate, except it was Angela staying out late or not coming home at all. Add the peanut-shells and you had a dangerous mix. Andy was just disappointed that the husband had come home and spoiled his entertainment.

"Damn bad timing. God-damn-cocksucking-motherfucking bad timing."

Andy liked his Americanisms, although Ham doubted whether Americans spoke like that outside of *Die Hard* films or *The Sopranos*. Andy's favourite was "Eat kerb sucker"

77

which he used at every opportunity. That particular one got him into trouble last year when he stopped a car for speeding and ordered the driver to eat the proverbial kerb. When the businessman – who was late for a very important meeting – got back up, his suit was filthy. He sued the Force, and Andy got a reprimand. It seemed that his colourful language hadn't upset the businessman but the dirty suit had cost him a lucrative contract.

"Never got chance to see her threepennies. In all the time we've been parking there that would have been the first time."

Andy sighed. The woman's previous shows had stopped short of removing her underwear. He felt that a great opportunity had been missed.

Ham said nothing, concentrating on the windows of Stockman Avenue, which were thankfully in darkness. For the moment his enthusiasm for seeing the worlds on the other side of those windows had been blunted. He drove slowly down the tree-lined avenue, negotiating the grassed mini-roundabouts that were a complete waste of time. Gridlock was not a problem in this quiet residential area. His radio beeped three times and the operator's voice cut through the silence. Ham felt static run up his arms and neck. The voice was sharp and full of tension.

"Location please. All officers stand by. Alpha Six. Radio's been forced into clear. Just give your location."

Ham stopped the car, waiting for a direction. Ahead or back.

"…Alex Pub, Albion Row."

It was Bob McFalls and he sounded out of breath. They could hear shouting in the background then Bob's radio cut out. More bleeps.

"All units, three code zeros at The Alex Pub, Albion Row. I repeat, three panic alarms. Officers need assistance. Units to respond please?"

Andy gave their call sign but it was drowned by another flurry of panic alarms.

78

"All units expedite. Three more panic alarms."

Blue lights and siren cut through the night as Ham spun the car round. The Alex was behind them and down the valley. The faster he went the narrower the avenue became and Andy gripped the handle as the right hand bend threw them to the left. He just had enough time to throw his call sign into the ring before Ham hit the mini-roundabout.

"Shit."

Andy wasn't sure if he still had the transmit button down or not. The car mounted the shallow kerb then scored a path across the grass before taking off over the rise. The wheels touched down with a bump.

"Fucking shitty death."

Andy abandoned the Americanisms for more local expletives. Visions of Ham's encounter with the tree branch and the ditch flooded his mind and he wished he'd never asked about Barney Koslowski. The avenue curved left and Andy braced himself for the turn. Ham faded right to give him a straighter line, eased off the accelerator, then floored it as he cut the corner. The wheels bit, steadying the car, and they were into the next straight. Another mini-roundabout rushed at them. Whoosh. Clang. The exhaust grounded briefly then they were heading towards the T-junction at the end doing sixty miles an hour.

Andy said a silent prayer as the give-way sign came into view, vowing to wrestle the keys off Ham after meal. Then they were out of the junction and flying, barrelling down the main road towards The Alex.

*

Considering it was half-past one in the morning the scene outside The Alexander Hotel was more reminiscent of kicking-out time on a Saturday night. If Stephen Spielberg had seen it he might have re-shot the beach landing for *Saving Private Ryan* because it couldn't live up to this. Four police cars were abandoned at various angles across the road and pavement, blue lights blazing, and the divisional van was half up the fountain the landlady had built to raise the level of her clientele. The fountain hadn't worked and her clientele were fighting in lumps all across the beer garden. There was blood and snot everywhere.

When Ham and Andy arrived X-ray Delta Nine-Eight was setting his dog after a runaway. Ham slammed the brakes on, skidding to a halt just behind the van, but didn't get out. He'd seen police dogs in action before and knew that the best place to be when one was on the loose was nowhere near it.

When Ham had been a probationer with eighteen months' service Eddie Sandford – a veteran dog handler whose German shepherd, Savage, was even less stable than Eddie – used to practice on young constables. During the nightshift at the Judges Lodgings – a duty nobody enjoyed because it meant sitting all night in the security office while Savage growled and tried to eat you – Eddie badgered him into wearing the padded sleeve so the dog could have a chew. Ham could vouch for the force of Savage's bite. The padded sleeve wouldn't stop you being bitten by a hedgehog never mind a rabid dog.

At about that time there had been a fight outside the Chinese Take-away at Meanwood bus terminus. Customers from the nearby chippy decided to argue the case for haddock and chips twice with scraps, over sweet and sour pork with rice. Too much beer turned the discussion into a daggers drawn punch-up, and a group of pensioners waiting for the last bus home called the police.

When they arrived there were clumps of wrestling drunkards all over the pedestrian precinct, the manager from the Chinese trying to kung-fu anyone that came near his window, which had been broken three times in six months. He didn't have the technique, only succeeding in pissing anybody off he chopped. Blood flowed from his squashed nose. Dan Hewlett, who owned the fish and chip shop showed more sense, simply locking the door and drawing the shutters.

It was take-your-pick when it came to making arrests, and Ham chose the smallest combatant, who proceeded to beat the stuffing out of him. After a struggle he got the midget handcuffed and rolled him under a patrol car so he wouldn't get run over by a passing bus. The pensioners tried to flag it down but the driver wasn't stopping anywhere near the bus stop. Instead he made the mistake of leaning out of his cab and asking Eddie Sandford if he needed any help. Savage saw the sleeve and thought, *Judges Lodgings*. Showing remarkable restraint the dog only ripped the drivers sleeve off, barely breaking the skin.

To cap it all, the pensioner who called the police got arrested for being drunk and disorderly. The bus driver complained but nobody knew which dog man had been on duty that night.

X-ray Delta nine-eight's dog wasn't like Savage. If ever there was dog whose bark was worse than its bite it was Gummy. The ex-guard dog would have trouble working at Mothercare. Still, Savage scarred Ham for life, so he stayed in the car.

Two officers from the neighbouring division were chasing a skinny man wearing a white baseball cap across the green. The dog man called them to stop and set Gummy loose. The dog raced past the two policemen and made a beeline for the running man. The dog barked and slavered, giving a good impression of being vicious. The man glanced over his shoulder, looking worried. Another two yards and he would have probably given up but he didn't need to because Gummy decided to take a leak. He stopped dead, sniffed in a circle around the centre of the green, and then cocked a leg. The man got his second wind and crossed the road into the estate. Savage would have turned in his grave.

Ham got out and took stock before wading in. Andy was already dragging an overweight man with a beard off an equally overweight woman. Both had flobby men's breasts but his were shapelier than hers. As far as Ham could tell the only difference between them was the beard. The woman's was less pronounced. Amid the chaos and shouting a familiar cry went up.

"Eat kerb sucker."

Andy yelled into Mr Flobby's ear. He didn't have much choice because before he could respond Andy had one arm up his back and was grinding his face into the pavement. The rigid handcuff snapped onto one wrist and Andy was trying to get the other arm round when Mrs Flobby came up off the ground like a bullet.

"Get off him you skinny bastard."

"Wha…"

Andy was knocked sideways by a tidal wave of flesh, losing his grip on the cuffs. The man rolled onto his back and swung a meaty fist that narrowly missed Andy's nose. The handcuffs, sticking out from the wrist like an extra limb, caught him on the cheek and instead of eating kerb Mr Flobby looked like he was going to eat Andy. His wife was ready to help and in about thirty seconds Ham's tutor was going to be an Andy sandwich crushed between opposing forces of hot sweaty flesh.

In the distance sirens approached from all over town. Every division had received the flash message. Officers need assistance. When the balloon went up it was all hands to the pumps. It had been that way ever since Ham joined. Savage wasn't here but the scenario was the same. Groups of wrestling bodies. Blue lights flashing. Grunts and curses from bobbies and prisoners alike. This was the battle of Chip Shop Hill all over again.

A seething mass of tangled bodies shouted and screamed at each other around the fountain. Instead of improving the Alex's clientele it simply gave them something to fight in and three women were trying to tear each other's hair out while getting soaked to the skin. On such a warm night that would have been quite pleasant if it wasn't for the pain. Their blouses were plastered to their breasts, peanut-sized nipples pointing accusingly, and that would have been quite pleasant too if Ham didn't have to rescue Andy.

Andy missed the nipples altogether. Great walls of flesh were crushing the breath out of him as Mr and Mrs Flobby-Men-Breasts attacked each other again. He was wedged between them and watched the rigid cuffs flash past his nose three times before he managed to grab hold of them again. It was time for Ham to join in.

The woman was on top and you didn't have to be a rocket scientist to know she was far too heavy to pull off on his own. Ham moved in behind her and went straight into the Koslowski technique. He hooked his first two fingers up her nose and pinched with his thumb. Once he'd got a good grip he twisted and pulled.

"Eeeeoowww…"

"Gerroff her."

A great weight rolled off Andy as the woman followed Ham's lead, slithering to one side like a beached whale. Ham bent over her.

"Put your right hand behind your back."

She began to argue so he twisted her nose. The hand flew backwards. Ham quickly released her nose and snapped one cuff on her wrist. He now had something to lever with and kept the wrist cocked so she couldn't move it.

"Now. Other hand."

With her nose free she found her voice again.

"You're for it."

"Other hand. If you want to keep your nose."

A twist of the cuffs and she complied. He snapped the other one on and double-locked them, then twisted her into a sitting position. It wasn't easy moving so much weight but at least the leverage of the cuffs forced her to do most of the moving herself. Another two cars and a detention van pulled up and five officers got out. Two came over to Ham and took the woman from him. He shouted after them.

"Drunk and disorderly."

"I told you to eat kerb, mother-fucker."

Ham turned to Andy who was trying to screw the man's hand off with the handcuffs. Being almost crushed to death did nothing for Andy's humour and he suddenly realised he was missing the nipple show in the fountain as well. That was it. The stream of invective coming out of his mouth bore no relation to what he would write in his pocket book later. Before Ham could get his bearings Billy Hollis shouted across the crowd to anyone who would listen.

"Somebody take over. I'm losing it."

In the entrance to the beer garden Ham saw the tubby constable kneeling on top of a teenager with more tattoos than a military band. Billy held the lad's hair in one fist, pounding the head into the concrete path. Billy's voice rose to a squeal, a trait that always embarrassed him, and his cheeks flushed bright red. Just behind him a bottle smashed against the wall.

"I'm losing it."

Ham dodged between two women, one with legs right up to her shoulders wearing a skirt that left nothing to the imagination, and another who appeared to have no legs at all. She was so dumpy that standing beside the leggy brunette she looked like an amputee. Stumpy was warning the brunette to leave her husband alone. Just where her husband was Ham couldn't tell but he ignored them for now and pulled Billy off the prostrate form on the floor.

"Time out. Take a breather, Billy."

Ham turned the youth over, thankful that his brains weren't staining the pavement. Billy didn't so much have a short fuse as no fuse at all. His most famous transgression came at a domestic in Moorhead Crescent. The scruffy council estate was a breeding ground for no-necked cave dwellers, most streets having at least one burnt-out car and three boarded-up houses. The telephone wires were cut twice a month and whenever they stayed up were decorated with old bicycle tyres and the occasional pair of trainers tied together. The last place on earth you should send Billy.

It was dark when the call came in and, hearing that they'd

sent Billy single-crewed, Ham and Andy turned out to back him up. They arrived shortly after the shit hit the fan. A brain-dead turtle of a man from number eleven had the temerity to question Billy's parentage. That was the wrong thing to say because a lack of pride in his family was not one of Billy's shortcomings. He was intensely proud of his mother and father, and was desperate to have children of his own. His wife was having a rough time with her pregnancy; so mentioning his family at all was suicide.

Billy hadn't been able to cuff the man and was manhandling him to the patrol car when Ham arrived. A crowd gathered at the end of the cul-de-sac, watching the entertainment. Turtle-man had been arrested so many times that it hardly warranted missing *Coronation Street* but even they knew that if Billy came for him there was going to be fireworks. They stood chewing sandwiches as if at a family picnic, all protruding foreheads and eyes-too-close-together, and watched The Police Channel instead.

Andy went inside to speak to the caller and check if there were any offences other than cheeking Billy after dark, and Ham opened Billy's door. The man was still muttering about the unfairness of life when Billy bent him in two to fit the car. Billy's technique wasn't to push the head down and say, "Mind your head," but to thump him in the stomach. Once he jerked forward Billy pushed him into the back seat.

"Twat. How'd they let a lump of potato in the police anyway?"

That was another mistake. Billy resembled a knobbly King Edward and was constantly ribbed at the station for looking like Mr Potato Head. That, coupled with a lack of height, gave him a serious inferiority complex. He worked twice as hard as anyone else, and Ham had to admit that he would do anything for you. Statements, enquiries, second jockey for interviews. Anything. But put him in the same room as an angry prisoner and he saw red. Put him in a car with an angry prisoner and the red was usually blood.

"Why don't you shut your stupid slack mouth?"

Billy climbed into the back of the car and drew his hand-cuffs. Fearing the worst, the man backed into the far corner and stuck his legs against the front seat so Billy couldn't get near him. Billy tried to kick the legs away but there wasn't enough room to get any weight behind it.

"Put your legs down."

"Put 'em down for me."

The fuse had long since burned down. Billy held the rigid cuffs by the central bar and started to lace into the unfortunate prisoner.

"I said…"

smack

"Put your fucking…"

smack

"Legs down."

The man fought back but from a weakened position. With Billy leaning over him he rained blows about the man's head and shoulders, raising lumps and bumps all over the place. The car rocked like a caravan on shag-a-thon night. The picnickers stared open-mouthed through the back window of the car. It was like watching a widescreen TV in the garden, the mad policeman beating the shit out of the innocent prisoner. They knew that Mr Turtle was far from innocent but that didn't spoil their entertainment. Police brutality would have been on the tips of their tongues if they'd known what brutality was.

Outside the Alex, Ham checked the youth's head for lumps.

"What's he been locked up for Billy?"

Bob McFalls was shouting at someone in the beer garden but Ham had to concentrate on Billy who was sitting against the pub wall hyperventilating.

"I don't know."

"Nowt. That's what," the youth said.

Ham could smell beer and vomit on his breath, so drunk and disorderly was looking good. Whenever there was a pub fight you couldn't go far wrong with D and D. He'd never quite got his head round the other public order offences since coming out of Scenes of Crime.

"Only called him a chicken nugget."

The youth rubbed the back of his head. Ham looked at him.

"Well. Under Section 4(5) of the Practical Policing Act 1875, using inappropriate chicken language after dark is an offence. Colonel Saunders would turn in his grave. Handcuffs, Billy."

Ham handcuffed the lad using Billy's cuffs and was about to get him up when a shriek went up behind him. He spun round in time to see the leggy brunette take a punch in the mouth.

"Ya bitch, it's your fault," the shorter woman said. "Ma man's locked up."

The brunette reeled then hammered a closed fist on top of the woman's head. Then it was all legs and fists as the women clawed at each other over the affections of the tattooed youth on the floor. Seeing him being beaten half to death by Billy didn't seem to have bothered them but the handcuffs proved too much. The mini-skirt got shorter and one breast popped out of the boob tube. Andy was missing everything tonight. Both women crashed to the floor, which at least evened up the height advantage, and then the wife ripped his lover's hair right off. For a moment Ham was shocked, certain there would be blood all over the pavement, then the wig was thrown clear and the women went at it again. The youth groaned.

"Oh fuck. Take me away. I'll admit to anything."

Billy got up, apparently recovered, and Ham led the youth away from the melee. Billy even managed a laugh, although it seemed a little ragged. He took over and nodded his thanks. The two women were tearing lumps out of each other but it seemed to be an even match so Ham left them to it. He'd learned long ago that there was nothing as dangerous as trying to separate warring females. Providing there were no weapons involved the best thing was to let them fight it out of their systems and then lock them up after.

Ham looked around for Andy and saw him trying to coax the wet T-shirt contestants out of the fountain. There was no let up in the combat round the front of the pub, groups of battling partygoers trying to gouge each other's eyes out or kick seven bells out of one another. Bob McFalls shouted again, his voice coming from the beer-garden, and Ham remembered it was Bob who'd sent out the first alarm. He went through the wrought iron gate into the garden round the back.

At first he couldn't see anything. The lights had been turned off, just the overspill from the streetlamps lifting the darkness in patches. The crowd who had been fighting here had moved out, joining the melee near the fountain, and the secret garden was engulfed in an eerie silence. The trees and bushes that surrounded the lawn soaked up the shouts from outside, turning the garden into a quiet backwater. Ham looked around but couldn't see Bob. He was about to go out, assuming he had been mistaken, when Bob called again.

"Mick. Over here."

Ham didn't know where, "Over here" was. The voice seemed to be coming from everywhere, not grounded in one place at all. Blue flashing lights intermittently penetrated further than the dull orange sodium lights. They turned the lawn into a field of blue grass with bruised smudges of shrubs sprouting above the flower borders. Conifers formed a wall across the back and three apple trees that the landlady optimistically called an orchard stood to the left. She had no more luck with the orchard than she did with the fountain. Her customers weren't for calming, even if she'd installed a Tibetan monastery.

A bottle flew over the wall, landing harmlessly on the grass. Blue light glinted off it. There were no more sirens from afar; everyone who was coming was here already. If they didn't calm the situation down soon the police were going to come up short. For the first time Ham thought this could turn out to be dangerous. It surprised him. The one thing that had never worried him was the possibility of being injured on duty. Putting the uniform on made him feel invulnerable somehow. The fact that he had his stab vest, and his side-handled baton, and his CS spray gave him courage that wasn't normally part of his make-up. Off duty he was just as shaken as anyone else if there was trouble. His radio as well, that was the other thing that gave the illusion of safety, the ability to call on his colleagues to help him out. Except everyone was here now and they were still losing. And he still couldn't find Bob McFalls.

Another bottle thudded softly on the lawn, adding twin sparkles of blue flashing light to the scattering of coals. Coals? Ham looked closer, squinting in the gloom. Not coals, apples from the orchard. While he watched, another apple fell from the furthest tree and the branches rustled.

"Mick? What the hell are you waitin' for man?"

The tree shook and more apples dropped. The familiar Geordie twang broke into a stream of obscenities.

"Fuckin' shitty death man."

Ham walked over to the tree and looked up.

"What are you doing up there?"

"What do you fuckin' think? Apple kippin' aren't I."

The trees were taller than Ham thought, several branches forming a ladder to the higher boughs. Three steps up the dark figure of the world's unluckiest Geordie clung on for dear life.

Bob had fled the border counties after suffering for years because he had a Scottish name. The taunts of simply being a Scotsman with his brains kicked out from the people north of the border were marginally less offensive than the assertion that his family had kicked out of Scotland for being feeble-minded. Add to that the unfortunate fact that with a name like McFalls he was afraid of heights and he was saddled with more than his share of burdens. Joining the police force in the north of England provided little respite since a thick skin and a sense of humour were prerequisites for the job. "If you can't take a joke you shouldn't have joined," was the usual rejoinder to any sensitive soul who didn't like it.

"Is that why you pressed your panic button? Because you're stuck up a tree?"

Relief that Bob wasn't lying unconscious in the shadows washed away Ham's concerns and the absurdity of standing in a blue-washed garden in the middle of the night while half the world was fighting outside raised a smile.

"No it bloody wasn't. Now help me down."

"Where's your prisoner?"

Since Bob's was the first alarm to go off he had to assume he'd been making an arrest at the time. He was double-crewed with Billy and he'd already seen Billy's handiwork.

"Not up here obviously. Oh shit…"

Bob overbalanced and grabbed a branch for support but the branch was springy, almost catapulting him backwards. A shower of apples hit Ham on the head and shoulders.

"Watch it. I can't put an injury-on-duty in for being attacked by an apple tree."

"You'll be attacked by me in a minute if you don't get me down."

"All right. Hold on. I'm going to guide your foot to the next branch."

Ham took Bob's left foot and placed it on a lower branch but Bob didn't want to let it go. He felt more secure where he was than stretching down and shifting his balance, which was precarious at the best of times. He could fall over going up a flight of stairs, never mind climbing a tree. With a little coaxing he found another foothold, moving his grip back to the trunk before stepping down to the next one. The lower branches were stronger and with each step Bob felt happier. When he was on the ground he let out a sigh of relief.

"Better?" Ham said.

Bob nodded, embarrassed now that he was safely on terra firma.

"Bugger that bloody cat in future."

Ham understood then. Despite his hard-man-of-the-north image, Bob was a staunch defender of animal rights. He didn't throw red paint over women wearing fur coats or acid on Boots Chemist windows but give him a cruelty case and he was on it like a rabid dog. He was the unofficial RSPCA liaison officer and took a dim view of anyone treating animals badly. Up until now he'd drawn the line at climbing trees.

"If that landlady doesn't clean her act up I'm going to get her licence pulled."

"You all right?"

"I don't want this ending up in one of your books."

Bob ignored the question. He knew, as most of the shift did, that Ham wrote children's books in his spare time, and was paranoid that if he ever got one published someone would recognise Bob McFalls as the bumbling gargoyle or whatever he wrote about.

"Cats are very sensitive to local ambience. And definitely aren't conducive with pub fights and glassings. She's putting Leroy through a lot of stress. No wonder he always hides in the tree."

"Where's Leroy now?"

Leroy was the Alex's mouser, a black and grey tomcat that reminded Annie of a smoked-out drug dealer who used to be a customer until he shot-up once too often and overdosed. When she found him in the toilets at closing time he'd turned grey with patches of black. His dong was almost as long as the cat's tail so she changed the cat's name from Smokey to Leroy.

"Jumped down the minute I was level with him."

"He always does that, Bob. I don't know why you bother."

"He looked more frightened this time. I think it was the blue lights."

"Well, whatever it was tonight. I think it's about time you let him sort it out for himself. Or keep a ladder round the back. Now, where's your prisoner?"

"Billy took him out front."

"Yes, I saw him. Do you think it was a good idea to leave him on his own?"

"Billy can handle himself."

"I was thinking of the prisoner. You know what Billy's like."

"Sorry."

A window went through round the front of the pub, the noise snapping Ham back to the situation at hand, a near riot where the police were outnumbered three-to-one. Bob snapped to as well.

"Okay, that's enough. Bloody cat's going to have a nervous breakdown."

He stormed through the gate to save all creatures great and small from excessive noise and violence. Ham followed. Another divisional van had arrived and several prisoners were being manhandled through the back doors. The three women in the fountain had forgotten their differences and were happily stripping off to the sound of breaking glass from the pub. Andy was nowhere to be seen.

Finally, Inspector Samson pulled up with the station megaphone. It had only been used twice since Ham had been there, once to talk a jumper down from the railway bridge and once to wish Merry Christmas to the residents of Darkwater Towers, a block of flats near town that had been turned into an old people's home. The divisional collection had provided several food hampers that were delivered by the early turn shift on Christmas Day. Since then the bullhorn had gone missing and it took the inspector three-quarters of an hour to find it, but he was here now.

He lifted it to his lips and the speaker let out a squawk of static that tugged at everyone's fillings. It shut the crowd up quicker than anything he could have said. Another burst of static and people were holding their jaws in agony. Inspector Samson, a barrel-chested mountain of a man, gave up and shouted between cupped hands.

"Right then. Everyone stop fighting right now, or I'll bring in the O.S.U."

Ham doubted if any of the drunks knew what the O.S.U. was but the force in Inspector Samson's voice was so intimidating that he could have threatened them with Richard and

Judy and they would have still calmed down. The Operational Support Unit would have taken hours to call out but fortunately the mere threat was enough. The less violent members of the crowd drifted away while the rest disentangled themselves and dusted each other down.

After five minutes, all that was left was the landlady and the three women in the fountain who were down to their underwear. Any of the bobbies who hadn't locked up were standing round urging them on until the Inspector warned them to calm down as well. Ham stood beside him.

"Maybe we should just send you to disturbances in future."

"Could do for me. I miss it sitting in that office or going to meetings all the time."

"Privilege of rank."

"Hmmph."

Bill Samson looked at the carnage then turned to Ham.

"Haven't you retired yet, Mick? You shouldn't be out here at your age."

"Four years to go. Same as you."

"Yes. Can't come a day too soon."

"Oh I don't know. How many crowds are you going to get to shout at in the garden centre?"

"Very true."

The Inspector raised his voice.

"Right then, let's saddle up and move 'em out."

The women climbed out of the fountain but their admiring audience were already filing back to their vehicles. The first van was rocking from side to side and Ham could hear Mr and Mrs Flobby-Men-Breasts hurling abuse at each other through the partition. Andy was waiting beside the car. Annie shouted at the Inspector's retreating back.

"What about my windows?"

He spun in his tracks and bore down on her like a charging bull.

"You should have closed two-and-a-half hours ago."

"We were having a private party with a few friends."

"Fifty people isn't a private party. And if I check your till rolls I'll be closing you down. So don't push your luck."

One by one the blue lights blinked out and the parade of police cars, divisional vans, and Gummy's mobile kennel u-turned in the road and headed for the police station. As the last car disappeared Leroy sauntered through the garden gate as if nothing had happened.

*

The cell area looked like a tube station during the Blitz. There were prisoners waiting to be booked in everywhere and groups of police officers were filling in proformas with names, addresses, and arrest times. The more unruly prisoners were in holding cells where they continued to hurl abuse at their captors. Mr and Mrs F.M.B. were in separate cells. They had stopped swearing at each other and were now pledging their undying love.

There wasn't a single officer on the streets, the entire division having either arrested or providing statements somewhere in the cell area. The first three prisoners had just been booked in when another fight came in over the radio. A disturbance outside the Pizza Ranch just down the road. At this time of night they would be cleaning out and Ham had no doubt that some of the stragglers from the Alex would be arguing their case for a last minute pizza. Beer in, brains out. Worked every time.

"Sarge," Bob McFalls said. "Fight at the Pizza Ranch. Finished with us?"

"Any more from you?"

"No. Ours are booked in."

"Right. Off you go then."

Bob and Billy dashed out of the door and seconds later the squeal of tyres filtered through the concrete walls. A single blue flash through the window and they were gone. Ham looked at Andy.

"Trust Billy to be first out. Give it ten minutes and we'll have another war."

The custody staff ploughed on, notching up one prisoner after another. Five minutes went by and another two officers were free. Ten minutes and another two headed for the door. Ham looked at his watch. The radio blared.

"Any units free to assist at the Pizza Ranch? Reply with call sign."

"Told you," Ham said. Andy smiled.

More tyres squealed in the yard as the released officers went to back-up. There were just three more prisoners before Andy and Ham's. Listening to them you'd think you'd tuned in to *The Love Boat*. The vows of loyalty were flowing thick and fast. Ham loosened his stab vest.

"We'll do our books at meal time."

"Yeh. As soon as we've booked these in."

Ham glanced at the clock on the wall. Almost two o'clock. Perfect timing. After meal he could hand the keys to Andy and get rid of his stab vest, which had been irritating him all night. The excitement should be over for a Sunday night and they could coast towards their two days off without incident.

The radio crackled again.

Ham's heart went cold and for a second he felt as if someone had walked over his grave. No message came over the radio, just another two bursts of static. The custody sergeant waved the next prisoner forward. They were next in line.

"Any unit free for an immediate?"

The urgency in the operator's voice said it all.

"Man with a knife at Hill Top Hostel. Any unit? Reply with call sign."

There was no reply. All the other officers were down at the Pizza Ranch. The custody sergeant looked up from his desk, sensing the urgency of the situation. The officer booking his prisoner in was tied up so that only left Ham and Andy.

"One of you stay with your prisoners. I can let the other go."

Ham had the car keys. He nodded at Andy, pulled them from his belt, and headed into the night.

Hill Top Hostel

Helen Elswit didn't expect to get stabbed any more than Mick Habergham expected his career to end before the shift was over. The well-lit windows of Hill Top Hostel looked in on a crowded office and the side windows of that office looked onto a cluttered reception area. It was the reception area that was the problem, the sliding window permanently open so residents didn't feel excluded. It also gave the residents free access to whoever was behind the counter.

Tonight that was Helen.

The school leaver was pleased with her first two weeks as a healer of the sick, seeing her role as a doctor of the mind. Her mother had raised Helen and her older brother Robin alone, teaching them to respect other people's life choices and not be judgemental. Her mother's life choices were made when Helen was too young to understand, ejecting her father in favour of a lesbian librarian with excellent spelling.

Robin was less forgiving, becoming staunchly heterosexual. He had even deepened his voice into a macho growl to rub Helen's nose in his maleness. Having learned everything she knew from books it never occurred to her that once his balls dropped his voice would drop too. In her mind the vagaries of approaching manhood didn't extend beyond raging acne and a smattering of whiskers. The electric razor their mother gave him was hardly needed because a stiff breeze would see his face hairless in a jiffy. It was a pity it couldn't do the same for his spots, which had erupted overnight somewhere between his twelfth and thirteenth birthdays.

Helen was determined not to be judgemental but that didn't extend to her brother. Robin tried hard to be the rugged out-door type but only succeeded in becoming more introverted. Having a lesbian mother – no matter how good her spelling – and a socially conscious sister did nothing for your street cred. Not having a father didn't help either. Helen was blissfully unaware of this, seeing her brother as yet another example of how men were dangerously unstable. She didn't know what unstable was until she met Marak Vargo.

Flo Avery, Helen's tutor and fellow night-worker, knew of him but they hadn't met. Vargo was an emergency referral, moving in two days ago after the police and the Department of Social Security couldn't house him before the weekend. He was given a room in the annex away from the single mothers and battered wives. There were a few dispossessed teenage boys but otherwise the hostel was mainly female. So were the staff, which made it a popular tea spot for passing patrols, Andy in particular. He drew the line at some of the pale and spotty mothers though. Their pallid complexions and skinny arms had more to do with the "H" plan diet than the Geri Halliwell workout. Drug rehabilitation was another of the hostel's criteria.

"Yes, but do you think she would really sleep with him?"

Helen put her coffee down and watched Flo perform a little pantomime with her cup before deciding it was too hot to drink.

"Well, she is Welsh. And the way she's been pushing her chest in his face I don't think she was offering to cut his hair."

Helen gasped. Political correctness was her byword, one learned from a long list of sociology books. Flo on the other hand had spent fifteen years watching the machinations of her female charges and knew that you could take the woman out of the man but rarely the man out of the woman. Especially since men had been getting inside these girls ever since puberty.

"That's a slight on *Helens* everywhere."

"If it wasn't for the cameras, Big Brother would be hearing the patter of tiny feet before they start the next series. And I doubt that Paul would be around to help."

"Now there I agree with you."

"Glad to hear it."

"He is definitely just looking for a holiday romance."

"I don't think romance comes into it."

"No. But you know what I mean."

"Yes. I see the result around here all the time."

Helen thought about that while she sipped her coffee. Most of the young mothers here were the result of broken homes and the boys who got them pregnant rarely offered more than token assistance. If any of them knew what contraception was she'd be very surprised.

Although Hill Top Hostel was a shelter for the homeless it was single mothers who filled most of the rooms, the few boys that stayed there being kept as far away from them as possible. The narrow corridor to the annex – "C" block, the girls called it, and it took Helen a week to figure out what the "C" stood for – was as much protection as they could offer. The presence of males caused tensions the girls shouldn't have to deal with in Helen's view. Helen's view of men was entirely one-sided and not at all flattering.

The front door banged shut, intruding on her thoughts. Then it banged again, and again. She went to the reception window to see what the commotion was and came face to face with Marak Vargo. Her opinion of men dropped right off the scale.

"Excuse me. Could you keep the noise down, there are people trying to sleep?"

The hunched figure with its back to her paused in mid swing, holding the door open with one hand while the other was hidden in the folds of his greasy black overcoat. Long straggly hair was plastered to his head and there was half a sandwich stuck on one shoulder. The sandwich had been there a long time. Vargo said nothing, turning slowly to face his accuser.

Helen's blood ran cold.

Marak Vargo was nothing like the teenage boys she was used to dealing with. He was thirty-five, with gaunt features and high cheekbones, and the dead white skin of a corpse. His eyes bore into her, leaking mucus that made them difficult to look at without feeling sick. He stared at her for a few seconds and then slammed the door shut again. Helen found her tongue.

"I said keep the noise down."

It was the wrong thing to say. Vargo's other hand came out of the folds of his coat; knuckles bone white as they gripped the handle of the knife.

*

"Go on, call the police. I want them to come for me."

His eyes might be leaking gunge but there was nothing wrong with his sight. He saw Flo reach for the telephone and knew she wasn't ordering pizza. Just as well since Pizza Ranch was up to its neck in fighting drunks and policemen. Helen's mind went blank, standing at the counter flicking through her internal index of "things-that-I-have-read" and coming up with nothing remotely like this. She had nothing to say and simply stared at him open-mouthed.

"I want them to come, and I want a lot of them."

Marak waved the knife. Helen could hear the phone ringing all the way from the police station, the sound coming down the wire and out of the earpiece. It seemed to be ringing forever. Her breath sounded loud in her ears. Deep inside the hostel there was only silence.

The phone kept ringing.

"Send them all. Every last one of them."

The blade swished again. Helen was frozen to the spot, her arms braced against the counter. She found herself thinking that Marak Vargo was the most polite knifeman she had ever seen, praying for someone to answer the telephone. Didn't they have some kind of call handling criteria? You know, answer the telephone within three rings for an emergency or one minute for all other calls? Even as she thought it she realised how stupid that was. How were they to know which calls were urgent? Her mind was rambling. Her eyes mesmerised by the long silver blade.

"Come on, answer the phone," Flo said.

"Yes answer it. Send them all. The more the merrier."

The knife jabbed at Helen. She didn't feel threatened. Whatever was bothering him had nothing to do with her. He was obviously peeved at the police for some reason, or perhaps it was just authority figures in general. That thought kicked in another. Yes, this was a classic case of rebelling against authority, usually springing from a deep-rooted hatred of the father figure. She could relate to that, if she'd ever known her father.

"Why don't you like the police?"

Marak stopped swishing the knife and looked at her with rheumy eyes. At the other end of the wire someone answered the phone. Helen listened with half an ear, hearing voices but not words. She was about to make a giant breakthrough.

"Why don't you like authority?"

Helen was about to make a bad situation worse. She thought she was getting to the root of the problem but what she said next triggered the explosion.

"Why do you hate your father?"

The knife flashed out and the pain was instantaneous. There was no blood at first, just a cut in her blouse, then it soaked the material and flowed down her arm.

"Send the police. And they'd better come armed because I'm going to kill one of them tonight. I'm going to kill you as well."

*

Ham covered the three miles to Hill Top Hostel without wearing his seatbelt and the feeling of insecurity took him back to the ditch, and the tree branch, and Barney Koslowski. That night he'd felt a lack of control as he sped along the country lane because he rolled one way on the bends then swung back and rolled the other way.

Barney played an important role in Ham's development, including the first time he'd come up against a mad knifeman. That had been during the summer of 1976 and it wasn't a knifeman but a knifewoman. She was carrying a twelve-inch shard of broken mirror instead of a knife. And she was naked.

When they arrived at the report of a woman trying to kill herself she was on the first floor landing. Her husband stood in the doorway at his wits' end. Ham went in first while Barney locked the car – the previous day they'd attended a burglary only to find three kids playing cops and robbers in the patrol car when they came out. Ham thought the husband was missing a few grey cells upstairs but that was nothing compared to the problem he had upstairs in the terraced house. If his marbles were loose then his wife's were completely lost. She pranced around the landing waving the makeshift dagger and mumbling incoherently. Her ribs and hips stuck out like an underfed greyhound's and the floppy folds of flesh that passed for breasts slapped skin. Even her nipples looked underfed. Blood ran between her fingers.

Ham's first concern was the blood. He'd seen dead people and dealt with road accidents but neither required him to wrestle with someone dripping blood. The possibility of getting cut himself didn't enter his head. The other thing that bothered him was her nakedness. Forget the blood. Forget the knife. Where do you grab hold of a naked woman to restrain her?

While he wondered what to do she ran down the stairs and

into the front garden. Ham shrunk back against the living room door as she passed then followed her outside. As far as he could see she hadn't cut herself apart from where she gripped the piece of glass. There were no slash marks on her wrists or throat. That was good but Ham didn't know what to do as she ran around the tiny square of lawn with the neighbours looking on. Barney didn't help, standing at the front gate laughing. Barney laughed a lot.

Ham took positive action. He held his arms out as if herding sheep and dodged from side to side trying to pen her into one corner. This tactic failed miserably because every time she came near him he backed off, the sight of her floppy breasts disgusting him. The shard of mirror began to look less threatening than the possibility of having to touch her clammy flesh. Barney had seen enough. He came into the garden, grabbed the woman round the waist and took the makeshift knife from her. She struggled but had no strength, waving her arms and legs as he carried her under his arm to the car.

Ham felt out of control tonight as well, and not just because he wasn't wearing his seatbelt. The feeling that there was no safety net invaded his thoughts. There would be no Barney Koslowski to laugh and take over. Nobody to help at all. Everybody was fighting drunken pizza men, or booking prisoners in.

For the first time in years the comfort of the uniform wasn't enough. The night was a large and empty place when you went into battle and its silent corridors hid sleeping people who didn't even know you existed. They would wake up in the morning refreshed, unaware of the conflicts played out just down the street, or across the road. Ham clung to the hope that the message was exaggerated. That was always possible with the new call-handling system. You could end up talking to an operator in Glasgow before the message was passed to your local police station. Ham had lost track of how many immediates he'd attended only to find he was at the wrong address. Local knowledge wasn't good when you needed an interpreter two hundred miles away.

He had been to one call that came in as a domestic assault and damage that got completely garbled in translation. After racing up the garden path because the wife had been bottled and the front window smashed, Ham was confronted by the happily drinking couple belting out Elvis songs on the lawn. The window had been smashed when they got locked in and couldn't find the key – something they couldn't find with their singing either.

Hope of that faded when he climbed out of the car in front of the hostel. A woman was screaming in the office and through the glass doors he saw a shadowy figure lunge forward. A guttural voice growled and the figure lunged again. There was another scream, from two women this time. Ham looked through the window as he ran to the front porch and his blood turned cold.

*

Helen's arm was completely red now, blood dripping in heavy splodges from her fingertips, but at least she had regained her motor functions. She jerked back from the counter, splashing blood on the linoleum floor. Flo slammed the phone down at the sight of the blood, grabbed the tea towel from next to the kettle, and dashed to Helen's side.

"Get me the bloody police. All of them."

Marak circled the lobby, growling at himself, the knife flashing out in widening arcs. The blade was edged in red.

"I want them all. The fucking lot. BRING 'EM ON."

Flo wrapped the towel round Helen's arm and it immediately turned red. She didn't think the knife had hit an artery because the cut was on the top of the forearm, but she'd never seen so much blood from one cut. It looked bad and she wished she'd called an ambulance as well as the police. While she attended to the cut she saw a car pull up outside but there were no flashing lights. No sirens either. Marak didn't notice, too busy berating himself and life in general.

"The bastard. I fucking killed him. I hate myself. What a month I've had."

Someone got out of the car but Flo could only see one. The lack of blue lights worried her. On television they always squealed to a stop with blue lights flashing and sirens blaring. It just seemed more dramatic, as if they meant business. How much business could they mean sending one man?

"What are you looking at? Bitch. You're as bad as him."

The knife whipped towards them and Flo realised they hadn't moved far enough from the counter. She yanked Helen away, and almost fell over a typing chair, the wheels scurrying across the lino. The blade cut a furrow in the counter and both women screamed.

"I want to kill somebody. I want to kill myself."

He pointed the knife at his chest.

"Policemen. I'm going to kill a policeman. Two policemen. Where are they?"

He spun in tiny circles like a dog chasing its tail, the blade slicing through the air. His voice grew deeper, becoming a low growl as he lost all semblance of rational behaviour. His polite enquiries became shouted ramblings, interspersed with swear words he didn't even know he knew.

"Coppers. Where's the coppers?"

He had his back to the front door when it opened behind him.

*

Ham was glad he'd turned off the blue lights half a mile from the hostel. He hadn't needed the sirens. Years of experience told him that there was a time for sirens and a time for the silent approach. If it was near the end of your shift and you wanted the nuisance kids to be gone-on-arrival, sound them long and hard. If you didn't want a mad knifeman to gut you before you got out of the car, then softly, softly.

He saw the figure circling in the inner vestibule and waited outside. The porch door was closed, giving him a two-door cushion before he'd have to tackle the man with the knife. Judging by the blood he'd seen through the office window he had already struck. The threats left him in no doubt who he wanted to slice up next. Ham stepped away from the door and called code six down the radio. At least the log would register his time of arrival. He just hoped it wasn't his last time of arrival.

He turned the handle of the outer door and nudged it open an inch. The night was so quiet that any creak from the hinges would sound like a buzz saw. He winced then sighed as the door opened quietly. Silent approach.

Ham walked to the inner door, keeping to one side in case the knifeman could see through the smoked glass. The threats were coming thick and fast now, hardly muffled at all by the remaining door. The two-door cushion was down to one and Ham was glad he'd left his stab vest on. It covered his chest from waist to shoulders but left his arms bare. With the heat of the night he was wearing a short-sleeved shirt and his arms felt vulnerable. Any slash of the knife would open his flesh.

"Fucking coppers. I'm going to slice them up."

Ham tried to remember the layout through the door. He'd been here several times for domestic assaults or harassment, walking through these doors and into the office on the right, but hadn't paid much attention. He knew it was a small lobby between the office counter and the corridor to the TV lounge. The staircase ran off that corridor somewhere, but which end he wasn't sure. The problem was that the man wasn't contained. From the lobby he had access to both floors and most of the rooms. If one of the girls came down to see what the commotion was he'd have another target. The office door was always locked but the counter window open. At least one person had already been stabbed and Ham couldn't wait for it to happen again. He waited until the shadow moved away from the door then risked a quick glance. The door opened an inch then quickly shut again.

Ham sucked in his breath. In the words of Crocodile Dundee, "That's not a knife, *this* is a knife." He had been hoping for a lock knife, or at worst a flick knife – he didn't think he'd be lucky enough for the man to be threatening staff with a butter knife – but this was a great big, fuck-off, kitchen knife. Twelve inches of honed steel at least.

This wasn't Ham's usual, *this-glass-is-half-full* scenario. This glass was empty.

"I'm going to carve them up. The bastards. Like I did him."

Ham flexed his fingers to get the circulation going. He hadn't realised but he'd been clenching his fists so tight that his hands were numb. The stab vest would protect his vital organs but a low or high strike could still do plenty of damage and Ham wasn't even on nodding terms with pain. He didn't want to get too friendly with it.

There was nowhere to hide in the porch. No shadows to lurk in. A single fluorescent tube burned the shadows away like the sun on an early morning mist, leaving Ham exposed in a glass vestibule with no cover. He might as well try to hide in a telephone box. The lights were on in the office, and in the porch, and in the lobby where the man waited to carve him up. He wanted to sneak up on him but was frozen like a rabbit in the glare of oncoming headlights. His chest tightened. The car was coming and it was going to hit him, no matter what he did.

Ham fingered the catch on his belt. The side-handled baton could be extended and held against his forearm but it wouldn't provide much protection against a knife the size of Ainsley Harriet's. That "high-block", "low block" stuff on his refresher course was all very well in the gym but Ham wasn't about to risk an arm with it here. He drew the CS spray instead. The world pulled in around him. A pulse began to thump inside his brain and his heart pounded like a trip-hammer. His palms began to sweat. For a moment he didn't think he'd be able to depress the trigger without squeezing the canister out of his hand. He couldn't breathe.

"FUCKING BASTARD."

The frenzy of abuse culminated in a final scream and Ham knew the lid was about to blow. The figure stood still, arms stretched forward, the knife pointing at the reception window. He didn't have his back to the door any more but there was no more time. No pouncing from behind. This was going to be a frontal assault. Straight up the beach.

"AAAGH…"

Without a word, Ham flung the door open and extended his arm. During training he hadn't been able to hit a barn door at ten feet, so he levelled the spray at the man's head with more hope than expectation. For a split second everyone froze, a complicated tangle of movement caught in the blink of an eye. Captured like a Kodak moment in the glare of the flash. Helen and Flo held each other at the sight of the lone policeman. Ham stood in gunfighter's pose, weapon extended for the shot. And Marak Vargo was stunned to silence at the arrival of the very person he'd been screaming for. A copper. An authority figure. His father.

Then the knife began to move.

Marak's eyes registered his target and swung the knife towards it. Ham gripped the canister. Helen tried to shout a warning but her voice had gone. Flo hid behind her.

Then everything happened at once. The knife came up to attack position. Flo hit the floor with a thud. And Ham squeezed the trigger. A stream of spray shot out of the nozzle – less like an aerosol and more a child's water pistol – and Ham hit the barn door full in the face. Vargo dropped the knife and brought both hands up to his eyes, squealing and wailing like a slapped child. The aggression evaporated in a flash.

"DOWN. ON THE FLOOR. NOW."

Ham kept the spray at Vargo's head, ready for any counter-attack, but the madman had gone. This was complete surrender. Whatever demons had driven him had fled and all that was left was a retched child crying for his father.

"Sorry. Sorry. Ow, that stings. Really sorry."

His eyes were red and sore, snot stringing out of his nose

like a liquid rubber band. He was fumbling about, rubbing his eyes. Ham kicked the knife aside.

"Get on the floor. Face down."

Vargo flopped on the floor like a boned fish.

"Arms and legs apart."

Vargo formed a cross on the floor, arms and legs pointing to the four corners of the lobby. Satisfied that he couldn't reach the knife, Ham quickly picked it up and tossed it through the reception hatch. The CS was drifting in the room, gassing Ham as much as the man on the floor. His eyes began to water and he forced himself not to touch them. Rubbing only made it worse. He pressed the transmit button but missed, fingering the stubby aerial instead. He tried again.

"Alpha Two. One, code 112. Can I have transport? He's been gassed."

He didn't wait for a reply, pulling the rigid cuffs from his belt. Already his fine motor skills were breaking down. His fingers knew what to do but were struggling to comply. He'd better get the handcuffs on quick.

"Put your left hand behind your back."

The figure on the floor moved one hand, stopped, then moved the other. Motor functions. Ham crouched to one side and tapped Vargo's left arm.

"This one. Behind your back."

The arm came round and Ham snapped one bracelet on the wrist. He held on to the centre bar to control the arm.

"The other one."

The other arm wavered, unable to find the right spot. Ham grasped the wrist but had no more success than Vargo. His eyes watched though a sea of fog. Finally he brought the two hands together but still couldn't get the wrist into the second bracelet. He couldn't breath. His throat burned. When the office door opened he panicked, forgetting who was in there, and would have gassed Helen if his hands hadn't been full. The junior social worker, who had learned everything she knew from books, guided Vargo's wrist into the bracelet and closed the cuff. Life experience was beginning to teach her a few more practical lessons. Ham nodded his thanks.

"Could you open the door please?"

She did and Ham tugged on the handcuffs, pulling Vargo into a sitting position. From there he got him to his feet and guided him outside. Blessed fresh air washed over his face. The tension drained out of him but the adrenaline made his knees weak and his hands shake. He sat Vargo on the front steps then joined him. The sky was clear, stars dotting the heavens. A gentle breeze had sprung up, finally taking the edge off the heat of the night. Ham felt like Sidney Poitier waiting at the railway station in that small southern town, expecting Warren Oates to order him to his feet at any moment. He took deep breaths and blinked his eyes.

"Turn your face into the breeze. It'll clear your eyes quicker."

The sad little man beside him did as he was told, tears and snot smearing his face. He was shaking. Clouds began to gather on the horizon, carried by the very breeze that was clearing Ham's head. Soon they would spread across the sky, blotting out the stars, but for now Ham stared at the constellations and waited for the van.

MEAL BREAK

Ecclesfield Canteen

By the time Ham booked Marak Vargo into the cells and reached the canteen it was almost half past two. Arriving at the hostel and disarming the knifeman only took five minutes but waiting for transport and booking him in took over half an hour. Doing the file would take another hour, creating a work to follow-up ratio of eighteen to one. It would have been even more if Ham hadn't witnessed the offence and therefore didn't need to interview him.

The rest of the shift was already in and judging by the canteen the fight at Pizza Ranch had gone well. Half a dozen pizza boxes lay open on the table while a group of anonymous rappers jiggled about on MTV. Billy was trying to push a complete segment of Spicy Hot One into his mouth.

"Hey up. It's gas-happy Habergham."

Billy sprayed pizza over Bob McFalls. It was accepted that sitting anywhere within a forty-five degree arc of Billy when he was eating was a serious mistake. He once splattered Bill Samson with egg during early turn, prompting the inspector to put Billy out on foot for three days. Foot patrol was all but extinct in modern policing and Billy hadn't liked it one bit.

"Someone put the knives away," he said.

There was a pause in the festivities. Everyone had heard the call come in and knew Ham was single-crewed. When the ambulance was called they'd feared the worst. The only sounds in the canteen were the jiggly black men on TV and the throaty roar of the cold drinks machine, which had a motor the size of a small airliner. It almost drowned out the rappers and that wasn't a bad thing. When Shania Twain was on it was a different matter, everybody liked Shania Twain, even if she wasn't an anagram of Shiny Twat.

Nobody asked how Ham felt and nobody congratulated him on disarming a crazy man with a very big knife. The looks said it all. Well done. Glad you're okay. Then the troughing continued. Billy managed to fit the segment in his mouth and Bob McFalls moved to the end of the table. Andy caught the car keys when Ham threw them, waving him towards an open pizza box.

"No thanks. I've brought sandwiches."

"Surprise, surprise."

Andy pulled a chair out for him.

"That's all right. I'll sit over here. Spicy-hot-one and salad sandwiches don't mix."

Ham sat at a table in the corner near the window, spilling his tea right on cue. It was as traditional as the little tap-dance with the Pringles box to get the crumbs out. He did that now and raised a cheer from the other table. Three constables from the next division looked puzzled then tucked into their pizza again. Pocket books were out and between mouthfuls Andy tried to get the chronology of The Alex fight straight.

Ham sat in the corner and fingered his sandwiches. Being gassed had dented his appetite but he didn't think that was the main reason. Talking to Marak Vargo on the doorstep had saddened him and he didn't know why. Listening to tales of woe was part of the job. Ham must have heard every variation of life's travails at one time or another and it hadn't bothered him until Vargo's story struck a chord. Not with his own life but Angela's. That didn't explain why it upset him so much tonight, Angela's past had been with him for years. Then again he hadn't been contemplating divorce until tonight. That brought it into focus.

The sounds of laughter isolated him even more. The canteen was clean and airy, all smoked glass and chrome. The shutters were down on the serving hatch but the vending machines buzzed loudly and the TV washed music over the tables. In the next room a snooker table and darts board waited for anyone with time. It was all very up-to-date. Very now. A far cry from the cramped quiet of Clayton Wood canteen when he'd joined. Sometimes he wished he could return to those simpler times.

He had met Angela in simpler times.

Ham loosened the stab vest and slipped it off. A weight lifted from his shoulders but not from his heart, and when he dropped it on the next chair he felt short of breath. Angela inhabited the same time frame as Clayton Wood Police Station. At least in the beginning. The Police Force had still been exciting and his future lay ahead of him. Angela was part of that future.

*

Angela's mother, Janice, had been beaten up again. That's why Mick Habergham went to her house in the first place. Despite the severity of her mother's injuries it was the enormity of Angela's nipples that drew his attention. Ham let Maggie deal with the victim while he tried to avoid talking to those twin points. It was true what they said; men wouldn't be able to look women in the eyes unless they developed eyes in their breasts.

The back-to-back was small but tidy and Angela's mother was staying with her after the assault. It was a short-term solution. Janice got assaulted once a month no matter who her current boyfriend was, giving the impression of being a perpetual victim. It wasn't until much later that Ham saw her true nature. Angela had lived with it since birth. By the time Ham and Maggie left he'd already decided to call round again.

Once Angela's mother moved back home the back-to-back became a regular tea spot when he was on foot patrol down the valley. He often swapped beats so he could see her. Response times and immediate calls were unheard of back then and police work was more leisurely. An officer patrolling his beat had time to interact with his constituents; chew the fat; have a cup of tea; find out who was doing what to who and why.

He also had more time to spend at Angela's if she was home.

Ham lived five miles away in an attic bedsit. He didn't have a car and travelled everywhere by bus. After he'd taken Angela out a few times it was obvious they would become a couple and he spent many evenings at her house instead of his flat, walking home in the early hours. The quiet of the streets in the middle of the night intrigued him, a fascination that stayed with him all through his career. Even flying from job to job with Andy hadn't dampened his love of the nightshift.

Ham's favourite TV programme at the time was *When The Boat Comes In*. He sang the theme song with a Geordie accent all the time. Unfortunately the Geordie sergeant on the shift thought Ham was taking the piss and watched him closely for any infringements. Ham asked for time off to watch the programme one late turn – there were no videos then so he had to watch it or miss it. The sergeant turned him down so Ham went to Angela's for a cup of tea, a cuddle, and fifty minutes of TV. Two minutes before the programme started the sergeant called him on the radio. Ham ignored it. He called again, asking for Ham's location for a visit. Ham turned the radio off.

"You can't do that. What if he finds you?"

"He doesn't know where you live."

That was true, but he wasn't a sergeant for nothing. He listened to everything and forgot nothing. He knew Ham was seeing someone down in the valley and mingled with the shadows hoping to catch him.

"Anyway. Nothing should come between a man and his true love."

"You love *When The Boat Comes In* and these."

Angela jiggled her braless breasts, nipples pointing at the TV, and he had to struggle to watch the programme. He almost decided to divide his attention when there was a knock at the door.

"Shit."

Ham fastened his shirt and clipped his tie on.

"Hide upstairs. He can't search the house. Can he?"

"No."

Ham kissed her on the cheek and went upstairs. He heard Angela open the door followed by raised voices. She sounded angry but he couldn't hear what was said. The man's voice didn't sound like a Geordie. There was more arguing, then she called Ham down. There was a strong smell of petrol when he entered the room and a scuzzy teenager sat in Ham's place. He had "Love" tattooed on one set of knuckles and "Hate" on the other. A motorbike with the number plate snapped off stood behind the settee.

"This is my brother – Spencer."

The youth glared at him. Angela looked embarrassed. There was no kiss when Ham left and he wasn't sure what to do about the bike, which was obviously stolen. When the sergeant found him later Ham claimed he hadn't heard the radio calls but getting bollocked wasn't nearly as traumatic as meeting Angela's brother.

*

Angela's past was revealed slowly, the closer they became. Her nipples might have been the display that drew him but it was her unselfish nature that he fell in love with. The extent of her sacrifice became apparent later. And the price she paid.

It turned out Ham had met her mother before, when she reported a burglary. Janice's house was neither clean nor tidy, in total contrast to Angela's back-to-back. The burglar had climbed in through the kitchen window then gone straight to the cellar where he screwed the meter. Almost eighty pounds had gone. The landlord would have to claim off his insurance to pay the electric bill that quarter.

When Ham examined the cellar he found it hard to believe that any burglar could spend long down there. Janice owned a small rat of a dog and the cellar was its private toilet. Curled up piles of dog shit dotted the concrete floor, leaving barely a clear space to stand and the smell was overpowering. That cellar should have warned him what kind of family Angela came from.

And what she'd had to put up with.

The pieces fell into place over the next few years but matters didn't come to a head until the fight of eighty-six. Their own personal domestic. Ham couldn't put his finger on just what started the argument, whether it was her ex-boyfriend knocking on the door, or the visit by her brother and his friends. Whatever the reason it resulted in a broken hand and three months off work.

Angela was still living in the back-to-back and it was as tidy as always – her slide into laziness wouldn't come for several years – when Ham called round after work. He'd been late turn and didn't arrive until half past ten. She seemed tense, hugging him when he closed the door. He thought she'd been crying.

"What's up?"

He kissed the dark smudges beneath her eyes.

"Nothing."

She wouldn't meet his eyes.

"Then you've been crying for nothing."

"It runs in the family."

"Everybody cries. I cried at the end of *Von Ryan's Express* when Frank Sinatra didn't make it to the train. But nobody cries for nothing."

"I thought Frank Sinatra made it to the train."

"Only to the guard rail. They couldn't reach to pull him up. Then he got shot."

"Well, it could be worse. You could have cried when Bruce Willis blew up with that asteroid in *Armageddon*."

"I did. But don't tell the shift when you meet them."

Angela looked away.

"I'm not ready to meet them just yet."

"Aren't you coming to the Christmas do?"

She shook her head.

"Scared someone'll recognise your criminal past?"

Angela's eyes flared.

"I don't *have* a criminal past."

"Sorry."

Ham held up his hands in mock surrender.

"Look, something's upset you. What's going on?"

He held her in his arms and she laid her head against his shoulder. She led him to the settee and they sat down.

"I've been getting phone calls from my ex."

"He wants you back?"

"Yes."

"Well, of course he does. You're gorgeous. I'd want you back."

Angela hugged him but then another thought struck ice to his bones.

"Do you want to go back?"

"No. Silly. I want to be with you. He can be just a bit… awkward sometimes."

Ham was relieved. They held each other for a while then Angela began to undo his uniform shirt, kissing his chest. The discussion was over and she knew just how to put it behind them. She made love to him in front of the fire, riding him to climax, and talk of her ex-boyfriend was forgotten until they were in bed later. They were lying in each other's arms when the knock on the door came. It was loud and angry. A policeman's knock. At first Ham thought the sergeant had found him then remembered he was off duty. Angela looked out of the window.

"Oh no. Stay here."

She threw Ham's tracksuit top on and went to the stairs.
"Who is it?"

But he already knew.

"I'll get rid of him. Stay here."

She went downstairs. The living room light came on, slivers of yellow lancing under the bedroom door, and Ham went to the window. Keeping to one side he could see an American monster car parked opposite, all flash and no substance. It was the kind of car she'd told him Barry drove.

Raised voices from downstairs. An angry man and an even angrier Angela. Ham heard the word "Copper" used several times and the occasional swear word. He felt foolish hiding in a darkened bedroom while his girlfriend fought downstairs and was about to go down when the door slammed. Barry stalked to his car and sped off with a squeal of tyres.

Ham waited on the bed, beginning to feel angry himself. Why should he wait up here like a secret lover just because Barry couldn't accept that it was over between him and Angela? Why couldn't she just tell him not to come round again? That was the problem; she hadn't actually told Barry they were finished. Why couldn't she be straight with him?

After a few minutes the light went out and she came upstairs. Even in the dark he could tell she'd been crying again. His anger evaporated and he pulled her towards him on the bed. They lay in each other's arms and he felt sad. Seeing her upset always made him feel sad.

"Do you know you're the first person to hold a car door open for me?"

The question caught him by surprise but it didn't need an answer.

"You're the first person to make me feel special."

"You are special. To me."

"I think it was the flash cars that I liked at first. The fact that he's got the best clothes, and lots of jewellery. Women fell at his feet, and beautiful women too. I couldn't see what he saw in me. I didn't think I was good enough for him. Not as beautiful as the others. Not as clever. I was just glad he liked me at all."

"I haven't even got a car."

"You've got more than he'll ever have. I don't deserve you."

"Deserve's got nothing to do with it. You've got me."

"Have I? I keep expecting you to get bored and find some-one better."

"Better than what?"

"I'm not a good person. It runs in the family."

"You're good enough for me. Stop putting yourself down."

"I love you. I don't know what I'd do without you."

They made love again in the darkened bedroom, this time Ham taking the lead, teasing and pleasing until she reached an explosive orgasm. Afterwards they slept in each other's arms. Two hours later the stones hit the window and woke them up.

*

The pebbles rattled the glass but didn't break it. Ham was awake in an instant but Angela took a moment longer. This time he wasn't going to let her fight her own battles. If Barry wanted an argument he could have it with Ham. Another pebble hit the window and a voice called up.

"Angela."

"Oh shit," she said.

Ham recognised the voice. It wasn't Barry it was Spencer, Angela's errant brother. She went to the window then ducked back.

"Fucking shit. Why can't this stop?"

Ham was up and putting his tracksuit bottoms on when Angela held him back.

"Don't say anything. Please."

The panic in her voice tugged at his heart, hinting at a past he knew nothing about. She held his arms and looked into his eyes. Her face was pale in the light from the streetlamp. She looked like a ghost amid the shadows. Ham bit his tongue, holding back the words that could destroy them. It was one thing to fight over which TV programme to watch, or whose turn it was to do the shopping, but it was another to speak your mind about your girlfriend's brother. Blood was thicker than water, or love.

"I'm coming down as well. I'm not hiding up here again."

"But don't say anything. Don't lose your temper."

They went downstairs and Angela opened the door. Ham sat on the settee. The smell of petrol swept into the room when Spencer bumped the off-road bike up the step. He wheeled it behind the settee and leaned it against the wall. Spencer wasn't alone. A straggly-haired youth sat in the chair opposite Ham. His eyes were sunk into dark hollows and dirty black eruptions dotted his face. Not so much blackheads as black volcanoes. Spencer sat in the other chair and looked at Ham with undisguised contempt. He glanced at his friend.

"Giles. Can you smell something?"

Giles sniggered like an idiot schoolboy.

"Bacon. I smell bacon. Or is it Ham?"

For Spencer that was quite good. Giles sniggered again.

Ham gritted his teeth and said nothing. Angela closed the door.

"What are you doing coming round at this time?"

"Just passing. Weren't we, Giles?"

Giles appeared to have lost the power of speech, relying on grunts and sniggers.

"Well you can just pass someone else. And take the bike with you."

"Ooh, sis. Don't get a strop on. It'll only be here a few days. That's nothing new is it?"

Angela glanced at Ham then looked away. Giles scratched his head. Spencer just kept staring at Ham. Ham's blood began to simmer, not quite boiling point yet but getting there. The look on Angela's face earlier was the only thing that stopped him speaking up. The bike was dripping fluids on the carpet.

"You know, I could just do with a bacon sandwich."

Spencer was getting in his stride, his brain ticking off as many references to pigs as it could. All he could come up with was bacon so he played it to death.

"Nice crispy bacon. Short and curly."

"Spencer, stop it."

"Oink, oink."

Giles found his voice and joined in.

"Oink, oink."

Angela stood between them as if that would keep the sounds away from Ham. Her hands were shaking. She looked from Spencer to Giles then to Ham. She flicked her eyes upwards to the bedroom.

"No. I'm not running upstairs. Get these two out."

"Running with your little curly tail between your legs," Spencer said.

"That's it."

Ham lunged forward but Angela was in the way.

"Get them out of here, or…"

Ham's fists were clenched so tight the knuckles were bone white. If he hit Spencer now he'd likely knock him through the wall. Angela coaxed Ham towards the stairs then turned on her brother.

"Spencer. Please. Just go. Leave the bike, but just go."

"Whose side are you on? The police now?"

"I'm… I… Just go."

Giles stopped sniggering; perhaps realising how close Ham was to exploding. Spencer didn't care.

"Sleeping with the coppers now. Who'd have thought it?"

Ham was shaking, tension vibrating through his body, muscles tight as wires. Spencer slammed the door shut behind him, narrowly missing Giles as he darted through. The room reeked of petrol, an ugly stain spreading across the carpet. Angela's clean and tidy house was becoming less clean. Ham went upstairs and she followed, jumping when he smashed his fist into the bedroom door. The panel split. He roared his anger then thumped the door again. The panel pushed through, trapping his scarred knuckles. Blood ran down the paintwork. His fist was a twisted wreck. Angela rushed to him and held him tight. Her body hummed with emotion and he knew she was crying.

"Sorry, Ham. I'm so sorry. Please stop."

Ham couldn't speak, his voice tangled and shaky. He couldn't trust it.

"Please. Please. I'm sorry."

Slowly the tension eased. Her tears wet his shoulder. Their bodies were tied together but the knot was slackening. Eventually she risked a look at his hand.

"Oh, Ham. That was silly wasn't it?"

She kissed his knuckles.

"I can't move my fingers."

Angela led him to the bathroom and rinsed his hand. Two knuckles were cut and the entire fist swollen.

"Silly." Her eyes filled with tears. "I love you though."

Ham felt tears in his own eyes.

"I know. But…"

He shook his head. Angela touched his lips with her fingers, stopping him before he said something he couldn't take back. She sat on the bed and rested her head on his shoulder. The damp patch of her tears was already drying but there were more tears to shed. But not tonight. Tonight she sat beside him and explained about her family. The longer she talked, the colder Ham felt.

And the stronger his love for her grew.

*

Angela had one brother and two sisters. She was the eldest and their self-appointed protector. The mother who had spawned them provided nothing but pain and Angela frequently came between them and any punishments she meted out. When you have nothing but family, that family becomes everything. Angela wouldn't let them get hurt. The price she paid was a catalogue of beatings that would make your eyes water. The scars she acquired during childhood were constant reminders of a living hell that she could never leave behind.

The house with the dog shit in the cellar was their torture chamber and Janice delighted in torturing them. When their father ran away to sea to escape the witch that he'd married he left four young children with no protection except for Angela. Most of the time that was not enough.

Her earliest memories were of the smell. A dirty pissy smell they couldn't help because they had to live in the same clothes all week and sleep four-up in the same bed. The younger ones adapted well but Spencer and Angela bore the brunt of the abuse. The stress took its toll. Both wet the bed regularly. Since there were no blankets, only overcoats in the winter and bath towels in the summer, the smell of piss became so engrained that they couldn't smell it any more.

Everybody else could smell it though. At school everybody smelled it; at youth club everybody smelled it; and when they were playing out all the rest could smell it too. It became an obsession early in Angela's life to be clean. As soon as she was old enough to leave home she scrubbed the smell of piss out of her skin, destroying any clothes she took with her. She had no money, so getting new clothes was mostly by stealing. She didn't see anything wrong in that. After all, the people she stole from could spare a few clothes.

But there was still the problem of her sisters. Spencer moved into a life of crime as if born to it, staying with friends the minute he escaped Janice's hellhole. Suzie and Rache were still there. In order to protect them Angela moved into a rented flat round the corner, keeping an eye on them from her bedroom window. She didn't get any more scars from Janice because she was too big to hit but there were still scars to come, just not on the outside.

Sitting next to Ham, she fingered a soft white hole in her right shin. The tip of her finger fitted neatly into the dent up to the first joint.

125

"That one's from when she hit me with an iron bar because I told her boyfriend to leave Rache alone. He was babysitting." She laughed a short barking laugh. "He shit himself when I came in. I was trouble even then. Mum didn't though. She just swung with the bar."

Her fingers travelled up her thigh. A thin line of scar tissue ran across the meat at the top of her leg.

"A knife. I can't remember what that was for."

Ham said nothing, realising that she had to get this out of her system if they were to have any kind of future. He watched her hand touch the side of her head.

"I'm deaf in this ear. She stuck a pen in there. I think it was after she spent all evening crunching boiled sweets. Never offered any round, so I stole some for Rache and Suzie. That crunching... I couldn't stand it. I guess she decided to help me for once, made me deaf on that side."

Silver trails showed beneath her eyes. Ham curled up beside her, resting his head in her lap, and she stroked his hair as she spoke. It calmed her to have someone to look after. Suzie and Rache had gone bad long ago, just like her brother.

"It's not Spencer's fault you know. He turned to stealing just like I did. He just liked it more that's all. Still likes it."

She stopped stroking Ham's hair and he felt her body tremble beneath him. There was no sound but he knew she was crying again. After a while she told him how Spencer began stealing from her as well. He took her clothes from the washing line, and money from her purse, and finally started burgling her flat. He took everything she owned at one time or another but never stole from Rache and Suzie.

It was as if he were angry with her, maybe because she was the eldest and hadn't been able to protect them. He'd even stolen a ghetto blaster that belonged to her hard-man boyfriend of the time. Billy had beaten her to a pulp over that radio but she never told him who took it. The upsetting thing was that Spencer was outside when it happened. He could hear her screams as she cowered in the corner, taking punches, and kicks, and hammer blows with the kitchen chair. He even watched when the ambulance took her away. And she never told.

Family was everything to Angela. Wild horses couldn't tear her away from them yet they had removed themselves from her without conscience. Twice, when they had all been together under Janice's rule, Angela had been taken into care. Her mother cited unruly behaviour, but what she really wanted was a free rein with the kids. Angela ran away from the children's home, and later the secure unit, always coming home to protect her siblings.

Now, Angela's sisters ignored her unless they wanted money and Spencer used her as a halfway house for stolen motorbikes. The only justice was that Janice's choice of boyfriends meant she got beaten almost as regularly as she had beaten Angela. Small consolation in a twisted world.

*

The canteen was getting noisier. Shania Twain was on MTV, strutting her stuff in a leopard-skin jump suit. It might not have impressed her much but it definitely impressed the men sat beneath the television. Andy was drooling. The three officers from the next division chanted in unison. All sang along out of tune.

Angela's world faded but Ham couldn't forget the time, many years later, when it began to intrude on their own world. The life they had built for themselves out of the ashes of her past. It was when they were talking about buying a house together, a big enough step for Ham but a giant leap of faith for Angela.

They were shopping in town, Angela scouring the charity shops for bargain shoes she didn't need. Her tidy back-to-back was already becoming swamped by a tangle of shoes by Dolce and Gabana, or Versace, or whichever designer makes she couldn't resist.

"Angela, you've only got two feet. You'll have to wear a different pair of shoes every day for three years to get through the ones you've got already."

"You can't have too many shoes."

"Not if you're a caterpillar. And you're not."

"I know. I can't help myself."

"We'll have to buy a house with four spare rooms just to fit them all in."

"Well don't buy one then. Stay where you are."

She stalked off towards Help The Aged. Whenever the conversation turned towards the house purchase she always had a snappy put-down. The nearer they came to the exchange of contracts the more distant she became. It didn't take a genius to realise she was having second thoughts. With Angela, second thoughts manifested themselves in more shoes, or a nasty word. There had been a lot of nasty words lately.

She always managed to provoke an argument with the minimum effort. When he stayed at her place she would often keep him waiting for hours before coming home and sometimes she didn't arrive at all. It was a portent of things to come and it frustrated him so much that it was usually him who broke the relationship up. In a fit of temper he would tell her they were finished and the hard-faced bitch simply watched him go. Hard-faced when he was there. As soon as he left, the tears came. She was too stubborn to ask him to stay and knew deep inside that there was no hope for them anyway. Once he knew everything he would leave her, so it was better to make a clean break.

Stubborn she might be but Ham loved her. As angry as he felt, he spent many a night composing letters to push through her letterbox. She took him back amid floods of tears and apologies. And he didn't understand any of it.

He caught her before she could buy any more shoes and slid his arm round her waist. She tensed and he knew she was close to tears. Ham was bemused.

"I don't know what's going on with you. Don't you want to live with me?"

She didn't say anything but he could sense an explosion coming. He walked her to the park and they sat on a bench. It was autumn, the trees already turning from golden brown to yellow. Fallen leaves crunched under their feet. Ham was coming to the end of his tether. He didn't understand her and, as much as he loved her, wasn't sure if he wanted to put up with the pain.

"Do you want to call it a day?"

Angela nodded then shook her head. She shrugged her shoulders.

"You won't want to stay with me."

"Not if we stay like this, but I love you. Why can't we…"

The words wouldn't come. This felt like the end. Her words were heavy with hidden meaning. There was something deeper going on inside her head.

"No, you won't. I haven't told you everything."

Ham's heart went cold.

"Well, what more can there be?"

She held his hand and squeezed.

"You've been really good for me. I don't know what I'd do without you. But knowing you… You know… and being a policeman and everything. You won't want to stay with me."

"Don't be stupid. How bad can it be?"

"Bad, for you. That's why I can't tell you. We need to finish. That's all."

"No. That's not all. Let me make my own mind up. But don't just say it's bad, and we're finished."

A handful of leaves drifted from the tree behind the bench. Ham could see every vein and blemish as they floated in the sunlight. He felt short of breath. His heart was breaking and he was sure Angela would hear it.

"I'm sorry for what I've done. It's not your fault."

"Don't do this." Ham felt tears welling in his eyes. "Don't end us."

Angela paused, took a deep breath, and…

"Any unit free to attend an immediate? Man trying to cut himself."

Ham looked at his watch. Three o'clock. Barely half a meal break. He looked at the sandwiches that he hadn't touched. Andy was already getting up. He waved Billy and Bob to sit down.

"Get your stories straight. We'll call you if we need back-up."

Ham pointed at the keys on the table.

"Your turn to drive. Don't kill me."

"You're joking aren't you? After what you've told me to-night?"

Ham felt the weight lift from his heart. It was better to keep moving when you were depressed and he realised he was depressed. Given half a chance he would probably sit wallowing in self-pity for the rest of the shift. Thank goodness for a busy night. Andy hooked his belt on and headed for the door. Ham followed, giving their call sign over the radio. The door swung shut behind him as he took the stairs two at a time. Back in the canteen his stab vest waited on the chair.

FINAL TOUR

The House of Pain

Booger Smith was probably the most inept suicide attempt in the history of suicide attempts. Even so, tonight he managed to produce enough blood to feed a flock of vampires, most of it smeared over the walls, floor, and windows of his ground floor flat. He looked as if he'd dipped his body in a vat of red paint.

Alan, his neighbour and sometime friend, watched Booger drag the broken plate across his chest and wondered how long the police were going to be. He had tried to take the improvised blade from him but wasn't that much of a friend that he was willing to get cut. The girl from upstairs, a chubby lass called Karen, danced and jiggled in the street like a demented jelly, waiting to flag down the emergency services as soon as they arrived.

Booger, whose real name nobody knew, had tried to kill himself twenty-three times. If he'd failed his driving test that many times he would have been banned for life. As it was, he continued trying to ban himself *from* life with a complete lack of success. He was so incompetent that he had once caught the bus to Scarborough so he could jump off the footbridge high above the south bay road. He had read about the number of suicides there in the paper and liked the photograph of the span, overlooked as it was by the majestic Grand Hotel. It seemed like a suitable place to end it all. Unfortunately he'd got on the wrong bus and ended up in Bridlington, a town so flat that jumping off even its highest bridge would only break your legs. Broken legs were not what he wanted. Alan tried psychology.

"Come on, mate. Look on the bright side."

"The only bright side is bright red."

Booger scraped another furrow across his chest.

"Come on. Stop it. Give me the plate."

"There's plenty of plates in there."

Booger pointed to the tiny cupboard the landlord had the cheek to call a kitchen. Calling it a kitchenette would be pushing it but the description Booger preferred was scullery. Skull. That had the right tone of finality.

"In the skulduggery," he added.

He had difficulty translating his thoughts into words. He set fire to his dinner once, torching half the curtains and a tea towel. He'd dashed upstairs screaming for a distinguisher, leaving Karen – who wasn't the sharpest knife in the drawer either – wondering what on earth he was talking about. It was only when the smoke filled the stairwell that she realised and gave him a bucket of water, the only fire 'distinguisher' the landlord provided.

"I don't want any old plate. I want that piece of plate you're carving yourself up with."

"Tough. This piece is spoked for."

"Aw, come on."

Karen bounced through the door like a demented space hopper, all flapping arms and bouncy flesh. Her eyes were rolling as if she'd seen a ghost.

"Where are they? Where are they? Oh my God."

"Look. Just leave me alone. I'm not hurting anyone. I just don't want to live any more. The rent's paid by social anyway, so nobody's out of pocket."

"Come on. Look on the bright side," was all Alan could say.

"The landlord will think that is the bright side. He's wanted me out ever since I ripped the cistern off the upstairs toilet."

One of Booger's more colourful suicide attempts had been in the communal bathroom at the rear of the house. That day he had been more determined than usual, reading about the deaths of outlaws in the old west. He'd left a copy of the library book open on the landing as a cryptic suicide note. A doublewide photograph of half a dozen gunslingers – who were as unsuccessful as Booger – stared up from the open page. They were on display in open coffins leaning against the local convenience store, the old west's answer to Kwik-Save.

Booger sat on the toilet and drank half a can of drain cleaner but all that did was make him sick and burn his throat. Plan "B" was to fill the bath, tie a fifty-pound dumbbell round his neck, and try to drown himself. Shoddy knotsmanship put paid to that one but the water he gulped down did help soothe his throat. In desperation he tied the washing line around the cistern and ran it through the landing window. Three more knots round his neck, then he jumped.

The knots were stronger this time, but unfortunately the cistern wasn't. His weight yanked it off the wall, spraying water all over the landing and ruining the book. Booger landed in the flowerbed, ripping his arms and back on the rose bushes. To add insult to injury he was charged for the book.

"That's not true," Alan said. "He gets the rent regular. What more does he want?"

"Bastard took my bond."

"Course he did. None of us to could use the toilet for a week."

"Alan. Just leave me alone. I'm not after an audience."

"Then why did you knock me up?"

"To say goodbye."

"You could have said goodbye in a note. That's what you're supposed to do."

"Lacks the personal touch."

"Look. Fuck off and give me the plate. I want to go to bed."

Karen danced about in the doorway but couldn't stand the

swearing and ran back outside. She didn't want the ambulance to miss them and sail right past. She even had a bright yellow handkerchief in each hand to flag them down. With a little effort she could have landed Concorde. Booger made one last plea.

"All I want is to be left in peace. Is that too much to ask?"

*

For most of Booger's life, that had indeed been too much to ask. Peace wasn't something that came easy to him. By the time he left school his temper had become legendary, causing him to be suspended three times and almost expelled twice.

His propensity for violence came out early, punching the milk monitor in the nose because he preferred orange juice. Any chance of being made class prefect quickly evaporated. Free milk was suspended by the government shortly after too, and most of the class blamed Booger Smith. Somehow the Prime Minister had heard about the milk monitor and decided to protect such potential civil servants by taking them out of the firing line. They secretly prayed that he would assault a dinner lady.

Even the classroom wasn't safe from his explosive outbursts. If anyone was foolish enough to flick ink-soaked blotting paper at him they had better be sitting near the door. He once walled up a potential rival for wolf-whistling at the supply teacher when Mr Radler was having his appendix out. Gary Hingely didn't know what hit him, and Booger never admitted what he used, but the surly bully needed five stitches and four weeks off school.

Despite his short temper, Booger wasn't a bully. He just reacted from a gut level when anything rattled his chain. In fact, by the time he left at sixteen, he had become a champion of the downtrodden masses. He disliked being taken advantage of, and very rarely was, but didn't like to see others taken for a ride either. If he saw some playground injustice he quickly levelled the playing field by taking the underdog's side. He often levelled the bully too.

For a boy who wasn't afraid of a good fight, his Achilles heel was the dentist. Booger was so frightened of the annual inspection that his mother took him to one of the new breed of dental practitioners, the psycho-dentist. Not only could you get your teeth done but have your phobias examined as well. Doctor Packard's favourite ploy was the distraction technique. He would hide his torture instruments behind your back while he soothed on about your latest holiday or the football scores. Once the drilling started, Booger's legs turned to jelly, flopping and twitching at every thrust into his mouth.

"Don't worry. Don't worry. This won't hurt a bit."

But it did hurt, and more than a bit. He could have given Booger a hundred injections – which were torture enough on their own – and he would still feel the drill biting into his teeth.

"Calm down. Just imagine you are on a beach. Beautiful sunshine. Warm Ocean. Swaying palm trees. You are on that beach. Imagine that someone else is in the chair."

It wasn't working. How could you imagine you were on a beach when the dentist had his hand in your mouth? The drill touched a nerve and Booger lashed out. He knocked two of Dr Packard's teeth out and threw the drill across the room.

"Imagine *you're* on a fuckin' beach. And someone else just got his teeth knocked out."

He stopped seeing the dentist after that, losing half his teeth to gum disease by the time he was twenty-five. He lost his mother by the time he was twenty-seven and his will to live by the time he was thirty. Unfortunately his foreshortened education left him without the skills to end it all, only allowing him to mess his body up and visit casualty departments across the county.

Romance was a problem because the few remaining teeth ruined his smile and after two days he beat the shit out of anyone who spoke to his girlfriend. Bethany, his latest conquest, finished with him two days ago. And now his football team had been relegated. No wonder he broke the plate and started cutting himself. He dragged the shard across one arm for good measure, ignoring Alan's pleas. He was about to change hands and slash the other arm when Karen squealed outside. Through the window he saw the pair of yellow cloths do a cheerleader routine then flashing blue lights split the night.

*

"Oh shit. I've been here before."

Andy pulled into the kerb, narrowly missing a woman who was trying to land an aeroplane, and turned the blue lights off.

"Doesn't look like he's tried to hang himself this time."

Ham looked at the splashes of blood on the front window.

"Ruined his lace curtains though."

"Police? Police? Where is the ambulance? I called the ambulance."

Karen continued to wave the yellow handkerchiefs even though they had landed, obviously expecting Concorde at any minute. Andy got out first.

"They're on their way. Do you mind flagging them down when they get here?"

"Well, when will that be?"

"Any time now. Thanks for your help."

Karen stepped into the road so she wouldn't miss the ambulance, flapping the yellow hankies in case she got run down. Andy went up the path to the front door, Ham half a step behind him. With each step the window looked bloodier and Ham thought Booger must have done it right this time. He was surprised to see him sitting happily on the bed, slicing chunks out of his chest with a broken plate. He was humming a tune that was vaguely familiar. Andy set his jaw and crossed his arms.

"Your landlord's going to be pissed off about this mess, Booger."

"He's already taken my bond, so he'll just have to lump it."

When Ham came in he was shocked at the state of the room. The narrow hallway was clean and bare, laid with lino instead of carpet and painted antiseptic white. There were no pictures on the walls. A mop and bucket stood at the bottom of the stairs, reinforcing the squeaky cleanness of the place. Booger's flat was a different matter.

"Good grief. Andy, have you got any spare gloves?"

Andy shook his head, already pulling his last pair of rubber gloves on. Blood was the last thing you wanted under your fingernails before you went home. Ham looked round the flat again. The walls were splattered with dried blood, the lace curtains on the front window pebble-dashed with the stuff. The beige carpet was ruined, stained red where Booger sat. A trail of bloody footprints led from the kitchenette, reminding Ham of Bruce Willis in *Die Hard*, only Booger wasn't wearing a vest. He was stripped to the waist and red as a toffee apple. Blood oozed out of a latticework of cuts across his chest and down both arms. It dripped from his fingertips, adding to the stain in front of him.

"You going to come in the ambulance?" Andy asked.

"Nope. I'm happy right here."

"Well, we can't just leave you like this. It's in my contract."

"Listen to them," Alan said.

"Don't have to listen to them. Don't have to go with them either."

Alan moved nearer the bed but Andy stopped him.

"Sorry. I know you're trying to help, but I need you to stay back."

Ham watched Booger draw the blade across his flesh and for a moment was back with the woman running naked round the garden. Blood dripped from the hand that held the broken mirror and her breasts slapped skin in the quiet afternoon air. The broken plate didn't look as sharp and at least Booger had his trousers on. Ham decided that getting covered in suicidal blood wasn't in his remit and went into the hallway for the

139

mop. He could hear Andy trying to calm Booger down but the problem was Booger was already calm. He just didn't want to go to hospital.

"What's wrong with the hospital?"

"They want to keep me alive."

"That's their job."

"Well, don't take me and they won't feel bad about it will they?"

"But I'll feel bad about not taking you."

"Then you're in a Catch 99 situation then aren't you?"

"Never mind Catch 99." Andy was getting mad now. "You'll be on Route 66 when the ambulance arrives. The only thing you've got to decide is whether you walk to the ambulance or I stretcher you in."

"Put that away. You don't need that."

Ham picked the mop up, squeezed it out, and went back inside. Andy was drawing his baton, snapping the extension out with downward flick.

"You like living in the house of pain? Well here's some for you. Put that blade down and stand up. Now."

Andy tapped the baton into the palm of his hand.

"Whoah. Come on, stop that."

"Broken bones or gas?"

Andy raised one arm to show the CS pouch on his belt.

"Give over."

"I'm not getting covered in blood trying to wrestle you to the ambulance. So, either put that down, or it's this." Andy tapped the baton again.

For the first time, Booger looked unhappy. Killing himself was one thing, getting battered by an angry copper something else. Like the low bridges of Bridlington, broken bones weren't what he wanted. He started to get up, the blade still in his hand. That was when Ham mopped him into the corner.

"Stay put. Pottery class is over."

Ham slapped the mop against Booger's chest and pushed him back onto the bed. The water cleaned a spot on his chest, turning the red man into a Telly Tubby, all red except for his TV screen chest. Booger didn't know what to do. He'd never been restrained with a mop before. Andy burst out laughing and put his baton away.

Once Ham was certain Booger was going to stay put, he withdrew the mop, keeping it across his arms just in case. The tune Booger had been humming came back to him and without thinking Ham began to sing.

"I am the man... of constant sorrow,

I've seen trouble all my days.

I have bid farewell... to Old Kentucky,

The place where I was born and raised."

He cupped his hands and Andy joined in the reprise in a deep voice.

"The place where he was born and raised."

Booger smiled at his favourite tune, something he'd picked up from *Oh Brother Where Art Thou?* One of the few films that cheered him up. He repeated the reprise.

"The place where he was born and raised."

Ham put the mop down and changed tunes, clicking his fingers and dum-dumming the opening of Ben E King's "Stand By Me." When he reached the vocal he stopped and pointed at Booger, who jumped straight in.

"When the night... has come,

and the land is dark

And the moon... Is the only light we'll see."

Ham joined in and before long he and Andy were doing the accompaniment to Booger Smith's vocals. Karen came in, looking puzzled, and almost dropped her hankies when she saw Ham playing guitar with the mop and Andy and Booger singing away. If it hadn't been for the patrol car, the ambulance would have sailed right past.

Ham rode in the ambulance with Booger while Andy followed. It was only when they reached the hospital that anybody questioned the clean spot on his chest.

*

"Couldn't you have cleaned the rest of him while you were at it?"

The nurse was cleaning the blood from one arm with a wad of antiseptic wipes. As soon as she cleared a patch of skin blood seeped from the cuts and filled it in again. It dripped from his fingertips, exploding on the clean white floor in tiny red bomb bursts.

"I'm not sure if I'm medically qualified with the mop. As a defensive technique I'm okay, but I'd need a medical certificate for cleansing wounds."

Andy smiled at Ham.

"I don't know how you're going to explain that on the use-of-force forms. They're going to have to make a new ticky-box for you. The Habergham technique."

He forced back another fit of giggles. Andy had laughed all the way to the hospital and his sides ached. He considered asking the nurse to look at it for him.

"And they'll need a new box under protective-equipment-used. I don't think they've got mop on it."

Andy and Ham were sitting on the examination table in the small cubicle while the nurse tended Booger's wounds on a chair opposite. They'd just finished accompanying Booger in another chorus of "Man of Constant Sorrow" and the failed suicide attempt looked anything but sorrowful. In fact he looked happier than the nurse who was fed up with repairing suicide attempts. She secretly harboured a desire to show him how to do it properly next time, then it would be the coroner's problem, not hers.

Ham began to click his fingers and Andy dum-dummed the intro music to "Stand By Me." Their repertoire was limited to what songs all three knew. Booger joined in right on cue, singing about when the night has come, and swaying to the music.

"Do you want to cut it out, or I'll let you bleed to death?"

"I don't think I know that one," Ham said. "How does it go?"

Andy laughed and the nurse threw him a dirty look. His chances of having her look at his side were looking slim. Ham stopped clicking his fingers. He supposed if everyone waiting for treatment started singing it might get a bit noisy around the casualty department. The nurse looked up from her work.

"None of the cuts are going to need stitches. I'm just going to clean and dress them, then you can take him away."

"Take me home?" Booger asked. Ham shrugged.

"We'll see. You're still under arrest don't forget."

"When did that happen?"

"Right after Andy threatened to gas you and just before I mopped you into the corner."

That wasn't strictly true. Neither of them had told Booger that he was under arrest but needs must when the devil drives.

"Under arrest for what?"

Booger was becoming agitated. Ham wished the nurse had let them keep singing. It kept Booger's mind off what would happen next.

"For your own protection, and damage to a plate."

"It was my plate."

"All right. We'll drop the damage."

The nurse was spraying Booger's arm with antiseptic but the sting didn't seem to bother him. She slapped a piece of orange gauze on his forearm then quickly bandaged it in place. While she was tearing open another packet of wipes Booger spotted the instrument tray under the table. He leaned towards the display of blades and syringes.

"Back."

Ham planted his size ten boot in Booger's chest, pushing him back in his seat.

"Let her clean these cuts up before you get any ideas about new ones."

"Nice one, Ham. First the mop, and now the boot."

"It's not fair. Why can't I go home?"

Ham sat back on the examination table.

"You probably can. But because you're in custody we'll have to book you in at the station, check you out, then release you."

"Will I get a lift home?"

"Of course you will."

Another white lie but Ham didn't think now was the time to be arguing about how long Booger would be in the cells. He decided to use the distraction technique.

"So, what upset you this time?"

"Bethany blew me out."

"That's all? Your girlfriend left you?"

Ham treated it lightly but was reminded of his own dilemma. To divorce Angela or not? He wondered how he would cope without the woman he'd lived with for almost twenty years.

"And my team's got relegated."

Andy sympathised.

"Now that's more like it. But if you can change girlfriends, why not change teams as well?"

Booger was shocked.

"That's disgusting. I've supported them all my life."

The nurse finished the other arm and started work on his chest. In the middle of the clean spot was a size-ten boot print. It looked like a long face in the white circle of a red T-shirt.

She looked at Ham.

"I'm not sure how you stand ethically with this one. Discipline and complaints would have a field day with a boot mark on a patient's chest."

"Yes, but forensic will never match it up."

Ham spoke from experience. Fifteen years in Scenes of Crime gave him a position of strength. A smudged boot-print in blood was going nowhere. The witnesses might be a different matter.

"But you'd best wipe it off for me. Or we'll start singing again."

"Consider it cleaned."

Ten minutes later Booger was in the back of the patrol car. Andy was driving and Ham began to sing after all.

"I had a friend named Rambling Bob... used to steal and gamble and rob,

Thought he was the swellest guy around."

Booger recognised the song and joined in.

"Well I found out last Monday... that Bob got locked up Sunday,

They got him in the jailhouse way down town."

They rounded a corner and the police station came into view. As if the sight gave them inspiration, Andy joined in, and for a few minutes they were The Soggy Bottom Boys reincarnated. The car shook to their voices.

"He's in the jailhouse now... He's in the jailhouse now,

Well I've told him once or twice... to stop playing cards and shooting dice.

He's in the jailhouse now."

He was having such a good time that Booger didn't realise he was Rambling Bob until the custody sergeant took his name and address.

Monday: 04.05 hrs

A stiff breeze buffeted the car as they parked to do their pocket books. Ham got his times straight with Andy for the Battle of the Alex Pub, deviating only where they became separated. Andy didn't record the fact that he'd spent twenty minutes watching three half-naked women in the fountain and Ham didn't mention Bob McFalls getting stuck up a tree trying to rescue the cat. Other than that their accounts were faithful to the event and if read out in court would recall just the right amount of chaos while covering the points-to-prove. Namely that everyone was pissed and fighting, thereby constituting disorderly behaviour whilst drunk. Drunk and disorderly.

Ham was just starting his entry about Marak Vargo when Andy spoke.

"What were you saying about Angela?"

Ham paused with pen in mid-stroke.

"When?"

"Down by Quarry View Cottage. You said something about you and Angela."

Andy knew just what Ham had said and really wanted to leave well alone but Ham was his partner. Whatever the difference in their ages, he felt obliged to listen to his friend's problems.

"Nothing."

Ham wished he hadn't mentioned it now. It was his problem. He shouldn't be burdening anyone else with it. Andy persisted.

"I've split up from every girlfriend I've ever had. None left me. It was always my fault. I suppose that makes me an expert on divorce, even if I've never been married."

Ham closed his pocket book and looked at the rustling trees. The wind was getting up, bringing clouds that blocked out the stars. The temperature had dipped but it brought Ham little respite. The heat of earlier in the night was preferable to the chill that ran down his spine now. He loved Angela but didn't think he could put up with her any more. He'd never split up with anyone before, any break-ups being forced upon him, and that made it doubly difficult. He knew how hurtful that could be.

"I don't know what I'm going to do. I've never left anyone before."

"How long have you two been together?"

"Nearly twenty years."

"It must be something pretty serious then."

Ham thought about that. Yes, it was pretty serious but it was also very hard to talk about, especially to another policeman. What she had done was hard to swallow but it was even harder to share. He didn't say anything.

"I've always worked on the pebbles-on-the-beach theory myself. You know, there'll be another one you'll like sooner or later. Usually sooner for me. Actually, usually before I got rid of the last pebble."

Ham knew most of Andy's sordid history. It was common knowledge among the shift, mainly because he told everyone about it himself. He kept no secrets and told no lies. It was one of the things Ham liked about him. Andy was an open book. Ham, on the other hand, was a very closed one. He found it difficult to open up but if there was one person he could talk to it was his partner. Andy had steered him through the rocky waters of his return to uniform patrol. Taught him, practically from scratch, the routines and procedures that he'd forgotten during fifteen years in plain clothes. It had been hard but Ham felt that his renewed enthusiasm was due in no small part to Andy Scott.

"Well, I've only had a couple of pebbles. And this one's become sort of familiar."

"They say familiarity breeds contempt."

"It also breeds contentment."

As soon as he said it Ham knew that wasn't the case with Angela. His state of mind at the moment was anything but content.

"So why are you thinking of divorce? Is she sleeping around?"

The question stung like a slap in the face. He couldn't answer.

"Or are you sleeping around?"

Ham laughed. A short bark that had nothing to do with humour. He shook his head, not in answer but because the thought of someone wanting to sleep with him hadn't entered his head. Angela was beautiful and still young enough to turn heads, but Ham? The ten-year age gap was one thing but twenty-six years of dealing with the dregs of humanity had taken the edge off his sexual magnetism. If he'd ever had any. He marvelled at the ability of men and women to stay married. They were separate species joined by a mutual need. Whether that was companionship, or love, or sex, it didn't matter. Somehow they put aside their differences for the common goal and amazingly made it work.

The windows he had looked through tonight proved that point. The lives he had glimpsed briefly, and even interacted with, showed the diversity of feelings for the opposite sex. The Delbacaros were still together despite the attempts of Mulder and Scully to force them apart. The failed security guard with a dog softer than Gummy forged ahead and even his daughters had found romance. Admittedly with members of their own family, but, hey, live-and-let-live.

Trevor Garner was a different matter. Whether it was his first wife, who still loved him, or his present wife who didn't like the first wife at all, he still had a relationship of sorts with both of them. There was no accounting for taste and Ham wouldn't touch either of them with a barge pole but somehow Trevor made it work. Being three-sheets-to-the-wind most of the time obviously helped. Even their son had a girlfriend.

Then there was the love triangle at Quarry View Cottage. Ham didn't know their names but it seemed to him that the woman was making a point. She looked uneasy with the thief of the night, a lover of convenience, and appeared relieved when her husband came home. Another relationship that was still chugging along. Barely.

The couples at The Alex were simply pissed. Reason left the human brain in direct proportion to the amount of alcohol ingested. Having said that, even Mr and Mrs Flobby Men Breasts were pledging their undying love by the time they were put in their cells. If a relationship could survive a blood-and-snot bust-up like that then there was hope for anyone.

Booger Smith was proof positive that man was not supposed to live alone. Forget about the football team, it was the heartbreak of losing another girlfriend that continually pushed him over the edge. His lack of success on the suicide front was probably due to a hidden desire to try again. Perhaps he was such a pessimist that he had come full circle, being a sort of inverse optimist. Trying to kill himself on the surface, while deep inside always expecting another chance. Another pebble on the beach.

So, where did that leave Ham? He wasn't sure. All he knew was that they couldn't carry on like this. He had put up with her antics for long enough and now it was time to stop. Whether or not there was another pebble on the beach for him, he didn't care. Still, if Trevor Garner could put up with two wives who looked like the back-end of a bus then surely he could survive with one who was drop dead gorgeous? A sudden gust of wind shook the car and the thought was still-born.

The radio broke into the silence.

"Alpha Two. Could you return to 79 Chagrin Avenue? Report of another disturbance. Woman screaming in the background."

Andy started the car and spun it round, headlights scything across the trees. The wind whipped them into a frenzy and there was the faintest suggestion of rain.

"Damn. I knew we'd get called back there."

Ham fastened his seatbelt and wondered if Trevor Garner's fate reflected his own? Perhaps it was an omen.

79 Chagrin Avenue

Both Trevor's wives were beautiful now. Their natural camouflage of ugliness had been stripped away by eight pints of Carlsberg and five glasses of Johnny Walker, turning each into the beauty he had fallen in love with. Drink had that effect on him, getting him into trouble more than once.

During his short stint in the army he'd enjoyed the rare privilege of a single room. His comrades nicknamed it the Battersea Dogs Home, threatening to report him to the RSPCA if he didn't stop abusing old dogs, but sleeping with Bette the Greek was his low point. Proof positive of the distorting powers of drink. He met her in a hotel bar the night before Remembrance Sunday and to be fair you shouldn't call her a dog. To be fair to dogs. Bette made Winston Churchill look attractive and when Trevor sat at one end of the bar she didn't even register on the Richter scale. Not even a low rumble.

That was before he started drinking.

As the night wore on he seemed to drift up the bar without moving. It was like one of those fancy slide-zooms in a Steven Spielberg film, pulling the background in while keeping the point of focus at arm's length. The point of focus was Bette and arm's length wasn't nearly far enough. Nevertheless they found themselves talking, her overpowering scent almost choking him. It was hard to breathe and he wasn't sure if it was the perfume or her overwhelming ugliness. To combat the tightness in his chest he had another drink. Then another. And another.

153

Now she didn't seem so bad. In fact there was a hidden beauty in her face that he hadn't recognised at first. Her eyes – once you discounted the layers of powder-blue make-up – held a twinkle that was very becoming. Her lashes were full and rich, curling sensuously almost to her eyebrows. The narrow waist complemented the fullness of her bosom and her legs looked like they went on forever. Long and sleek and shaped for loving. He was hooked. At closing time she took him to her house, driving erratically in a rusty Morris Minor. It was Saturday night but he was surprised when the living room light was on and the sounds of a cavalry charge came through the door.

"Bed, you two."

Two scruffy looking boys slinked past on their way upstairs, heavy lidded resentment pouring off them. It was water off a duck's back to Trevor. He was being wooed by Venus de Milo with both arms intact. She fluffed the cushions on the settee and took off her coat. Tom Tryon led the *Seventh Cavalry* across a battered black and white TV in the corner.

Trevor didn't remember the sex but it must have been good because he was grinning like an idiot when he woke up. He was wrapped around the smooth white shoulder of a beautiful woman he barely remembered meeting. Static hissed from the TV. Yes, it must have been a pretty good night. Now all he had to do was get back to camp for the Remembrance Day parade. He yawned and took a deep breath. That was his first mistake. The sudden intake of perfume almost killed him. It was so powerful it could have stripped paint, reducing the lining of his throat by three layers. His mouth tasted like someone had shit in it. Twice.

He had to find out what time it was.

Looking around the gloomy living room was a revelation. What had seemed to be a passion palace the night before looked more like a war zone this morning. Stained clothes were piled on the chairs and there was a pair of battered plimsolls on top of the TV. The sideboard across the back of the room was stacked with dirty plates and a mug of tea had so much fur on top it looked like a germ garden. He couldn't find a clock. His watch was on the coffee table in front of the settee but it wasn't alone.

Trevor suddenly felt sick. His arm slithered away from the woman's back and he tried to distance himself without pushing off. He was naked, his skin crawling with tiny maggots of dread. What had he done? More to the point, who had he done it with? He was vaguely aware that the corpse beside him had no head then realised it just didn't have any hair. That drew his gaze back to the coffee table.

His stomach did a lazy turn and threatened to reacquaint him with everything he'd drunk last night. Next to his watch were two half full glasses. What they were half full of he wasn't sure but inside them… Another stomach cramp hit him hard. A lazy blue eyeball stared back from one glass and a set of dentures grinned at him from the other. Bette's wig sat on the table like an obedient puppy completing the cast of "Bring Me the Head of Bette the Greek."

He dressed quickly, put his watch on, and quietly asked the waxy back if she could give him a lift back to camp. She refused with a fart and Trevor was out of the front door quicker than Flash Gordon. The whole incident was distasteful enough but when he walked into the barracks his embarrassment was redoubled. Leary nudges and winks greeted him and half a dozen squaddies yelled along the corridor.

"Eh up. Looks who's been shagging Bette the Greek."

It should have stopped him drinking for good but it didn't. Sometimes it was better to see what you wanted to see instead of what was really there. What was really there tonight was two ugly women about to fight for his affections. Joyce and Shirley were squaring up to each other and it was going to be a battle royal. In his present condition they looked like a pair of bathing beauties preparing for a mud-wrestling contest. The fact that he was married to one of them and divorced from the other slipped his mind. Just what started the argument was beyond him as well but he was sure it tied in with Marty's return and a warm glow in his loins.

*

They all heard the squeal of tyres as Marty pulled up but nobody looked out front. For some reason the eldest son of the Garner, nee Finnegan, clan preferred to park in the next street, climbing over the back fence to reach the house. It was something the neighbours behind them complained about regularly but it made no difference. Trevor reckoned it was a deep-rooted criminal instinct from Shirley's side of the family although he could just as easily have learned it from Trevor's brother. If ever there was a crook in the family it was Pat. Stole the business from right under his nose.

Henry's shoulders sagged. He thought the evening was getting on an even keel apart from the simmering volcano of Joyce and Shirley. Auntie Alice had fallen asleep but the arrival of the Crimson King woke her up. She farted. Susie Q was back, having seen her boyfriend lodged in the cells, and poured herself another drink from the bar. Trevor was in the kitchen picking over the remnants of the buffet. His alcohol intake improved the food as well so he selected a curled-up tuna and mayonnaise sandwich and a squashed triangle of quiche. There were several dog hairs on the quiche from when it had been on the floor but he didn't notice. If he could sleep with Bette the Greek he could manage a dog-haired quiche. Wesley barked in the back garden then Marty waltzed in the kitchen door. Trevor looked up but Marty was looking for someone else. He found her tending bar in the living room. Trevor followed him in.

"The wanderer returns. The prodigal son. The…"

Trevor ran out of sayings.

"Ooh baby. Come to mamma. Stop these horrid people taking advantage of her."

Shirley was drunk and when she was drunk became gushy

with her sons. Wayne should consider himself lucky to be locked up; when his mother got gushy it could be dangerous.

"Get lost, Mam. Leave me alone."

Marty fended off her drunken advances, not wanting a slobbery cuddle from his mother, or anybody else. He was twenty years old and way past that sort of thing. It was almost as embarrassing as when she shouted, "Ooh look. That's my son that is," to her friends across the supermarket.

"Don't talk to your mother like that," Trevor said.

"You've got room to talk," Shirley said. "You let this hussy talk to me any way she wants. Can't keep her bloody hands off you."

"Who're you calling a hussy?"

Joyce was past understanding what a hussy was but coming from Shirley it must be something bad.

"It's not my fault he'd rather be with me than you."

"You lying bitch."

Shirley lunged at her but Henry blocked her way.

"Now then, girls. Calm down. This was supposed to be a family get-together."

"Yeh, well. It is a family get-together. I was married to him first and he wants to get together with me again. Don't you honey?"

"Get that fuckin' bitch out of my house."

"I'm the bitch that's been there before you. Slapper."

"Ladies. Ladies."

Henry was fighting a losing battle and Trevor left him to it, pouring himself another whisky. Carlsberg simply wasn't strong enough for this kind of confrontation. He didn't notice Marty lead Susie into the kitchen. Joyce did and she wasn't going to keep quiet about it.

"Who's he prodding now? Betcha can't guess."

Shirley watched the kitchen door close and got up. Trevor saw it too, his suspicions about Marty drifting to the front of his mind. That had been one of the things he'd argued with Pat about after his brother took over the firm. Shirley shouted

157

through the kitchen door.

"What d'you think you're doing?"

She could see very well what they were doing when she flung the kitchen door open. Susie was trying to drown Marty in kisses while his hands wandered over her breasts.

"Aw, not your brother's girlfriend?"

Trevor stood behind Shirley and it was the only time they agreed all night.

"Susie. What's up with you?"

The girl should have been embarrassed at being caught but if she'd been that sort of girl she wouldn't have been snogging her boyfriend's brother at a family party. She giggled, almost as pissed as Trevor.

"Dammit, you nearly buggered the business, now you're trying to split the family as well?"

Trevor hadn't forgotten the number of times Marty had stalked female staff at GSI, resulting in a high incidence of resignations. A hulking security guard had once threatened to punch his face in after Marty chatted his daughter up. Trevor thought he should have let him.

"Sod off. They're not married."

Marty left his hands where they were. Susie giggled again. Her eyes had gone and Trevor wasn't sure if she knew who she was kissing. Or if she cared. If drink could turn Bette the Greek into a bathing beauty, maybe it could change Marty into Wayne. Deep inside he didn't think so but was willing to grasp at any straw. The circles of deceit running through his family were long and tangled.

The other bathing beauty, Joyce, saw her chance and seized it with both hands. Well, one hand actually, which she stroked up the inside of Trevor's leg. She'd been with him long enough to know that he dressed to the left and sure enough her fingers found what they were looking for.

"You didn't have this trouble with me, did you love?"

Trevor perked up immediately. Something else perked up as well. It was true that he didn't have this trouble with Joyce because they didn't have any children to cause this kind of trouble. In his befuddled state he forgot the sort of trouble they did have, which was massive and long term. He began to think she was the lesser of two evils. Shirley was squaring up to her son and didn't see Joyce lead Trevor to the settee. She sat him down and brought him another drink. Henry was beginning to think it was time to go home; this was only going to get worse. Joyce sat down and stroked Trevor's thigh. Another cloud was brewing in the kitchen as Shirley quizzed Marty.

"That's twice you've dashed off tonight. Where've you been?"

"Mind yer own business."

Marty didn't want to discuss this in front of Susie.

"Who've you been seeing at three in the morning? And does her dad know?"

Susie's ears pricked up, proving that she wasn't as drunk as Trevor thought. She knew who she was kissing and now suspected he'd been kissing someone else as well. She stood back and pushed his hands away. Marty tried to smooth Susie down.

"What's up? She wasn't in anyway."

Tact and diplomacy wasn't his forte. As soon as he spoke he realised he'd made a mistake. He'd lied too. It wasn't that the girl hadn't been in; it was that her father was still up and their stupid dog kept barking whenever Marty neared the door.

"Who wasn't in?"

"Nobody."

Marty back-peddled but it was too late. Susie stalked into the living room, Shirley looking disappointedly at her son. She was about to tear him off a strip when she heard the wedding march through the door. Whatever anger she felt at her son was about to be turned against her husband. When she stormed through the door she couldn't believe what she saw.

Joyce had stopped stroking Trevor's thigh and had one leg across him instead. They were holding hands like a courting couple while their wedding played on the TV. The volume was turned up to drown the shouting from the kitchen. That was the last straw. Shirley saw red and barged past Henry, who was trying to protect Auntie Alice from being caught in the crossfire. He failed and she farted again as she was bundled aside. When Shirley grabbed Joyce by the hair Henry was already calling the police.

*

There was no doubt where the trouble was this time. Once Andy turned the engine off he could hear the screaming from across the street. Ham was out and over the low fence before Andy cleared the car. As he approached the front door he saw the garden gobshite down the side of the house. The youth ran into the back garden, slapped his forearm, and drove a fist in the air at Ham.

"Fuck you, the boys in blue."

Ham considered giving chase then heard a glass break inside. Andy joined him as he went through the front door. The two fat ladies book-ended the little boxer, each straining past him to reach the other. If Ham didn't act soon the poor man would be crushed to death. An aging tortoise of a woman, all nose and no chin, cowered on the settee. Her mouth was a crimped piecrust and her eyes stared in horror at the fighting women. Captain Sensible stood behind the bar, having decided that enough was enough. Susie Q was crying in the kitchen.

"Get that bitch out of my house," one of the bookends shouted.

"She goes. I go," the boxer said.

"See? I told you," the other bookend said.

Ham struggled for the names. Andy beat him to it.

"Trevor. What's going on now?"

"This is my house. It's none of your business."

"It is our business if it's disturbing the neighbours. We can hear this row from the police station."

"I want her out of our house."

Shirley stepped back, giving Trevor room to breathe.

"That bitch's after my husband."

"I've *got* your husband you mean."

Shirley swerved past Trevor and went for Joyce, nails flashing. The boxer dodged between them again grabbing both of his wife's hands before she committed an assault in front of witnesses. The old woman on the settee farted like a pricked balloon. Susie came out of the kitchen.

"That sneaky bastard. He's been sleeping with some tart from down town."

"Trevor has?"

Ham was confused. Trevor had two women fighting over him in the living room and now he'd been seeing another one down town? What was he drinking? Susie didn't answer, collapsing next to Auntie Alice on the settee. Andy tried to separate the combatants, dragging Joyce towards the easy chair near the front window.

"Come on. Let's sort this out without shouting."

Ham stepped between Trevor and Shirley. He noticed the wedding video playing to itself on the TV. There was no mistaking who the blushing bride was, and it wasn't wife number two.

"Right. Let's start by telling me who's married to who?"

Ham looked towards Henry for help but the most sensible man in the room shrugged his shoulders in defeat. The damage had been done. Too much drink and not enough thought had brought the evening to the brink of Armageddon. It would take a miracle to smooth things over and Henry was fresh out of miracles.

"He is *my* husband."

"He was *mine* first."

"Look. We're not here to listen to a load of tit-for-tat squabbling."

Ham was getting annoyed. It had been a busy night with umpteen prisoners and a ton of paperwork to complete. Add to that his home life was spiralling out of control and every time he tried to decide Angela's future some other dickhead got pissed and started a fight. He'd just about had enough. Either these people started listening or the bloody lot could get locked up. He pointed at Trevor.

"You. Who are you married to?"

"Me," Shirley said.

"But he wants to be back with me," Joyce said, getting up.

"You two shut it."

Ham's blood was beginning to boil. Andy saw it and pushed Joyce back down. He'd only seen Ham lose his temper once and that was enough. They'd been patrolling in the van that night, and had arrested four Asian youths for burglary at the local school. They fitted the description and were eating a kebab with their takings. A quick search of their pockets produced enough pens and pencils to stock a stationer's so they were arrested. In the back of the van the youngest began to cheek the officers, playing the race card right from the start.

"You only nicked us cos we're black."

"You got locked up because you're loaded with stolen goods," Ham said.

"Got them for me birthday. Better let me go."

"Button it until we get to the station."

"Or else what? Can't do nothin'. I got witnesses."

A smirk spread across his face. Andy glanced back from his driving and saw Ham's neck grow red. Ham was quiet but Andy sensed trouble. He put his foot down, hoping to reach the cells before it arrived.

"Come on copper. What ya gonna do?"

The other three looked nervous, edging away from their younger accomplice.

"Eh? What?"

"Lights out please," Ham said.

His voice was strained, barely holding back the anger. Andy turned the interior light off and in a flash Ham had two fingers up the lad's nostrils. He yanked him forward and twisted until he screamed. Fingernails scraped the membrane at the top of the nose, drawing blood, and Ham twisted the other way. Another scream. He pushed the lad back just as the light came on again.

"You need to keep your nose clean. Have you got anything to say to that?"

He had nothing to say for the rest of the night.

Andy feared for someone's nose now and tried to calm the situation down.

"All right. One at a time. Quiet for now please, ladies. Trevor. Talk to us."

"Yes, talk now."

Ham was trembling inside. He took several deep breaths and counted to ten but was afraid the fuse had already been lit, not by tonight's events, but by the trouble at home. Sometimes divorcing your life from the lives of those you dealt with was difficult. Tonight he thought it might be impossible. Men and women. Who on earth suggested they could live together? They were like chalk and cheese, not so much from different planets as different universes. Ham clenched his teeth, feeling the anger rising inside him. These people were morons. Why couldn't they just get on with their lives without having to argue, and fight, and make the whole thing worse by getting drunk? If they didn't like each other, why not simply walk away? What breed of person actually wanted to stir up trouble? But he knew there were plenty who did, plenty who thrived on the badness. They weren't happy unless someone was unhappy.

Hatred rose like bile in the back of his throat. He had been dealing with this kind of nonsense for most of his service, the cause and effect of drunken stupidity. If it wasn't that it was sifting through the aftermath of crime, either the victim's grief or the systematic examination of the scene. The hatred coloured his vision, darkening his perception of what was going on at 79 Chagrin Avenue. But it was doing more than that. It was colouring his view of Angela, tainting his memory of the woman he had once loved. Still loved but couldn't live with any more. Just like Trevor and his two wives. The boxer had to make a decision, Joyce or Shirley. Ham had to make a decision too and as he pondered that he realised the hatred was turning on him. Darkening his view of himself. Hating himself for what he was going to do after this shift.

"Who owns this house?"

"We do. Me and Shirley."

"And what do you want to happen?"

Shirley jumped in.

"I want that bitch out of my house."

"Well, I'm not going. Trevor wants me to stay."

"Don't push this, Shirl," Trevor said.

The badness at the back of Ham's throat spilled out. He was sick and tired of trying to get people to be reasonable when all they wanted to do was argue. There was only one solution.

"Right. That's it. Party's over."

He turned to the woman sitting beside Andy.

"It's not your house, so you're leaving."

"Why should I?"

"Because you're under arrest. That's why. How many hints do you need that you're not welcome here?"

Ham pulled her up and nodded to Andy.

"Take her out while I sort these out. Prevent further breach of the peace."

Shirley smiled at her rival, content that she had finally got rid of her. Trevor was having none of it. The entire evening had just gone tits up. Ham pointed at him.

"This had better be the last call we get here, or you'll all be coming with me."

Ham followed Andy outside just as another two units arrived. There were no blue lights this time, just two pairs of tired officers who wanted to catch up on the evening's prisoners. There were files to prepare, statements to write, and pocket book entries to make. Andy passed Joyce over to Bob McFalls.

"Stick her in your car will you? I think Ham's shaping up for some more."

Bob sat her in the back seat and closed the door as Ham came up the path. He stepped over the fence onto the pavement and avoided Andy's eyes. The anger was out in the open but it wasn't diminished. He didn't want to take it out on Andy.

"What yer fuckin' doin?" Trevor shouted.

Ham wouldn't have to take it out on Andy. Trevor was going to save the day. He stood on his side of the fence and glared at Ham.

"Yer can't take her, she's done fuck all wrong."

Trevor was squaring up for a fight and Ham was more than willing to give him one. They stood on opposite sides of the fence, neither giving an inch. Ham thought he should at least try to keep the situation manageable.

"She'll only stay until there's no likelihood of her coming back. No charges. Just to calm things down."

"Then you should have taken her."

Trevor jabbed a finger at his wife.

"She lives here. Joyce doesn't. Now go inside. You're disturbing the neighbours."

Several bedroom lights were showing along the cul-de-sac. A distant voice called for them to be quiet. A dog barked in the back garden. Trevor took no notice.

"They're my neighbours. I'll disturb them all I want."

Shirley linked arms with him, trying to pull him towards the house.

"Come on, love. Let's go inside."

"Don't love me." He pulled his arm free. "Look what you've done. Got Joyce locked up."

Ham was boiling again. Was there no end to this stupidity?

"Last warning. Shut up and go inside. Now."

"Don't you tell me what to do in my own garden. Fuckwit."

Trevor jutted his chin over the boundary, tempting fate. Fate took its chance. Ham grabbed Trevor's shoulder and yanked him forward. He overbalanced and had to step over the low fence or fall over it. When both feet were on the pavement Ham grabbed one arm and twisted it up his back, snapping

165

one cuff on his wrist.

"Not in your garden now. You're under arrest."

Trevor still had a couple of moves left from his boxing days and danced round until his arm was back out front. Unfortunately, the magical effect of alcohol, which had stripped away the layers of ugliness from both wives, had the opposite effect on his legs. The nimble hoppity-skip turned into a clod-hopping tangle of limbs and he hit the floor with a crash. If Ham had wanted him down he couldn't have done it better himself. Before the boxer knew what hit him he was trussed up like a Christmas turkey, both hands handcuffed behind his back. That should have finally shut the disturbance down but a scream from the garden said otherwise.

"Leave my husband alone, you grey-haired bastard."

Shirley clambered over the fence, all wobbly flesh and profanities.

"You bitch," Trevor said from the floor. "Look what you've done. Got us all locked up. I'll tell you what. When she gets out, I'm going with her. You can keep the bloody money."

"Nnooo."

Shirley bent to cuddle her husband.

"Trevor, please come back inside."

She ignored the fact that he was handcuffed, trying to pull him to his feet. When she saw the bracelets on his wrists she turned on Ham.

"You bastards. Why did you have to come?"

Ham was in no mood for any more arguing. He grabbed her arm and locked her up. With no handcuffs left he waved Billy over.

"Drunk and disorderly. Four twenty-five. By me."

Billy led her away, still screaming obscenities. Ham looked at the house. The only people left were Captain Sensible, Auntie Alice, and Susie Q.

"Anybody else want to come?"

The dog barked from round the side but nobody answered. Ham began to shake with the aftermath of his rage. At least he didn't have to gas anyone. The canister was still empty after Marak Vargo.

*

It took thirty-five minutes to book the revellers in, mainly because the two women were screaming abuse at each other across the holding cells. Ham stood guard over Trevor in the juvenile cell – the only room in the house – while Joyce and Shirley were processed. He leaned on the open door and let his pulse return to normal. Trevor had returned to normal as well.

"You're okay, you."

Ham ignored him, writing his pocket book up so that Andy could copy off him later. He had finally caught up with Marak Vargo and Booger Smith, who sounded much happier than when he last saw him. Booger's reedy voice drifted from the east wing, doing a Soggy Bottom Boys solo.

"I'm in the jailhouse now… I'm in the jailhouse now…"

It made you wonder if he was truly committed to ending his life or should merely be committed. He wore a paper suit with no chords or sharps. There was less chance of him killing himself in here than off the low bridges of Bridlington.

"No. Honest. You are okay. I'm sorry I shouted at you."

Ham looked up.

"Apology accepted. Now be quiet while I do my book."

Trevor turned his back on Ham and stuck his arms out.

"Any chance of you loosening these? They pinch like a bugger."

"If you'd been like this in the first place you wouldn't be wearing them."

Ham put his book away and flipped the keys over until he found the handcuff key. He stood to one side and released the furthest arm then stepped back, keeping hold of the other. Once the cuffs were off he reset the ratchets and holstered them. Trevor sat on the hard wooden bench that doubled for a bed.

"I know. What can you do though? Couldn't let you take Joyce."

He rubbed the circulation back into his wrists.

"Joyce would have been let out in a couple of hours, once she calmed down. Now you're all here, and by the sounds of it she's a long way from calming down."

Ham looked at his charge for a moment. Trevor's decision had been made for him but Ham's was still to be made. He wondered what made the ex-boxer tick.

"What are you going to do when you're let out? You know, you said some things back there. Could make it difficult in the morning."

"Couldn't be harder than the last few years."

"Would be easier if you didn't invite ex-wives to family parties."

"Very true. Wouldn't have been half as much fun though, would it?"

Ham laughed, thinking as much about his own situation as Trevor's.

"You'll be charged and bailed in the morning. Drunk and disorderly. Depends how much you've had to drink when that will be."

Trevor smiled a sad little smile.

"Could be a while then."

"You really going to go back to… Joyce is it?"

"Don't know yet. Have to see tomorrow. Depends how much money Shirley gets hold of if I leave. Bank cards are in both names."

Trevor looked Ham in the eye.

"You wouldn't think I was a millionaire would you?"

"Wouldn't think, and don't think."

Ham couldn't imagine any millionaires living in Chagrin Avenue. Couldn't imagine any marrying someone so butt ugly either. If Ham were a millionaire he wouldn't be putting up with this shit from Angela, that's for certain. Trevor drew his knees to his chest.

"Ha ha. There you go you see. Swings and roundabouts. My brother ripped me off. Didn't know he'd make me rich the back way."

Trevor explained all about the swings and the roundabouts.

*

"I never knew that being run over could change your life so much."

Trevor was sitting in the corner, head resting on folded arms. He seemed less drunk than he had all night. Less drunk than he'd felt all year. Nostalgia often came out of a bottle for him but not this time. This was deep-well nostalgia, stuff of the soul. He felt as sober as a judge.

"It was Pat who skinned me. Brotherly love didn't enter into his way of thinking. Took me to the cleaners, and I wasn't badly off even then. Me and Henry got the firm going from scratch, worked all hours to keep it running. Burglar alarms first. Siting and fitting them. Wasn't long before we had our own premises and had to take on staff. Bit of vanity, calling it Garner Security, but Henry didn't mind. He's a toff. Henry. Wouldn't mind if you shit in his pocket."

Ham remembered Captain Sensible and thought they had shit in his pocket tonight. He seemed completely out of place at the party. Perhaps this explained why he was there. Not so much a friend of the family as a friend of Trevor Garner's.

Trevor closed his eyes, remembering better times. Happier times. The time when two struggling young men clubbed to-gether to carve out an empire in the security field. Blood sweat and tears forged a link between them that could not be broken, not even by Trevor's family, and that family had tried its damnedest. If it wasn't Joyce trying to come on to him, it was Pat trying to oust him, wrestle control of a company that was growing more powerful by the minute. They were hard times but simpler times. Ham remembered feeling the same way about his early years in the police force. Foot patrol. School

169

crossings. Handwritten interview notes. None of this rushing from job to job like tonight.

"I could have bought and sold you back then."

"Nobody buys me."

Ham bridled at the remark. Why did people with money always assume that the police were for sale? He'd read about corruption in the force but never come across it. In twenty-six years nobody had ever offered him money to get off a charge. Maybe he wasn't important enough? Perhaps you had to be higher up the ladder to be worth bribing? The worst he'd ever done was slip in a few more replies to secure a conviction and that was only because so many crooks got off on technicalities.

"No. But I bet I could have bought your house, or your car, or your summer holiday to the Costa-del-sol. You don't believe me do you?"

Ham didn't believe him. He couldn't reconcile the image of a man living in a council semi with that of the wealthy man he was describing now. If you could buy a policeman's house then why not buy something better for yourself?

"I had a boarding house in Morecambe that was raking it in, and two nursing homes across town. If my mam and dad had been alive they'd have been looked after there. Good food and clean rooms."

"So what went wrong?"

Whatever Trevor might have been, he certainly wasn't rich now.

"Ah. Money and family don't mix. Never knew I had so many relatives."

The first one to crawl out of the woodwork was Pat, Trevor's long lost brother. They hadn't spoken since their parents were killed in a car crash. Pat had disputed the distribution of the family estate, which was hardly a fortune, comprising of an ex-council house, a rusty Morris shooting brake, and fifteen hundred pounds. Trevor got the house and Pat the rest. He even took the carpets and curtains. Trevor lived in that house ever since. Ham checked that they weren't due at the charge desk then sat beside Trevor. So, it was the family home. That explained why he was still living there although Ham still wasn't convinced that Trevor was being strictly honest. He just couldn't see him as a moneyed man.

"Things were fine for a while. Having Pat nipping at my heels put a bit of extra pressure on me, but otherwise… No. I was poddling on okay. Apart from the drinking. That got worse. Then me and Joyce fell out."

Ham didn't ask why. He knew that would come next.

"Fickle bitch took a shine to Pat didn't she? He was wheedling his way into the business and she was trying to do the business with him. Bloody hell. It was the money again wasn't it? If the firm hadn't started making it big Pat wouldn't have shown up. And without Pat… Well, Joyce… You know. We'd have been all right."

"And she's the one you're going to leave Shirley for?"

Trevor shrugged his shoulders.

"When I've had a drink I love 'em both. They're gorgeous when I'm pissed. And I mean, I'm no oil painting."

"Maybe when they're drunk, you look gorgeous to them."

Trevor laughed.

"Naw. What looks good to them is my bank balance. Weren't always the case with Joyce though. Met her when I had nothing. She just slipped into being a greedy bitch."

Ham checked his watch. It was getting late and Trevor was up next.

"Am I boring you? No, really… You're all right you are. Better than these young coppers. You listen, like you're interested."

"Just don't ask questions after."

"All them others want to do is lock you up. Get points on their score-sheet."

"I did lock you up."

"Yeh. But I deserved it didn't I? I'm sorry, mate. For shouting at you."

171

"How come you married Shirley?"

"Ah well. The wheels came off didn't they? Work I mean. Pat took over cos I was too pissed to carry on. Pissed all the time. Hardly remember splitting with Joyce. The divorce must have come when I was asleep or something. Don't remember marrying Shirley either. Main thing about her was that she seemed kind. Took care of me when I had nothing. Just the house."

Again Ham thought about Angela. She had nothing when he met her, just the back-to-back she kept scrupulously clean, a few sticks of furniture, and half a wardrobe of clothes. She wasn't at an all time low but she'd definitely had it rough. Ham took her away from that, giving her hope where there had been none, and a future where there had only been a day-to-day existence.

"Then Pat ran me over."

Trevor could barely keep the glee out of his voice.

"Knocked you down?"

"Broke both legs, shattered my pelvis, and dislocated my shoulder."

Trevor had been walking home one night when his brother came up the road in the firm's Range Rover. Trevor was staggering but he wasn't swerving half as much as Pat. The police weren't sure at the time if Trevor had stepped onto the road or if Pat had mounted the pavement. It was the dented wheel rim and rubber burns on the kerb that swung the claim in Trevor's favour. All Trevor could remember was lying in the road staring up at Garner Security International written on the Range Rover door. When he sued, it was GSI that footed the bill. Four years later his brother finally paid up. The security firm that Pat had stolen from Trevor made Trevor a millionaire. Five point two million pounds. Irony was writ large, if only Trevor understood what irony was.

"Swings and roundabouts. They took his driving licence as well."

Trevor stood up, excited now that his tale was told. He

staggered and had to sit down again. The room swam before his eyes and he thought he was going to be sick. Ham thought so as well and stood aside.

"Whoah. Keep your buffet. I don't want it all over the cell."

"Guess I must have had more than I thought."

He had. But it was the realisation of what all that money had brought him that made him feel sick. The family came out of the woodwork again, not Pat this time, but every nephew, niece, and uncle he'd ever had the pleasure of not meeting. Not to mention his first wife, two ex-girlfriends, and a rescued dog nobody else would take in. Even Auntie Alice, who he couldn't remember at all. The worst thing was Shirley. She quickly arranged for Trevor's bankcards to be joint accounts and moved both her sons in with them. No matter how much he tried to keep the peace, the house his father left him became a battle zone. The entire family turned into The Munsters.

"You locked us all up in the end didn't you?"

"Just about. Only Henry, the old dear, and Susie missed out."

"Oh I don't know. You missed that little shit, Marty. He'll be flying around in his car, trying to shag that lass from the Pelhams. Henry's a good mate though. The only one who's not after my money."

"Oh yes. The five million."

"You still don't believe me do you?"

"In a word. No."

Trevor rummaged in his pockets, found nothing, then searched his coat and pulled out a crumpled mini-bank statement.

"Split it into seven banks. This is the only one she can get hold of overnight."

He handed the statement to Ham.

"If I kick her out, that's as much as she can take me for until I change the others."

The printer was almost out of ink but there was enough for

Ham to recognise the account names. Mr T Garner and Mrs S Garner. He had to smooth the paper out to read the balance. £342,754. It wasn't five million but it was more than Ham had expected to see. More than the resident of an ex-council house would normally have in his bank account. Ham smiled and handed the receipt back.

"Swings and roundabouts."

"Just make sure that whoever knocks you down's not on social."

"I'll try and remember that."

The custody sergeant shouted through and Ham led Trevor to the desk. Once he'd been searched his property was listed as: one watch, one belt, two buttons, and twenty-five pence in change. A crumpled piece of paper and a Kleenex were thrown in the bin. The sergeant looked up from the list.

"You won't be catching the bus home, if that's all you've got."

"The walk'll do me good."

"Don't spend it all at once." Then to the gaoler, "Cell, M5."

Monday: 05.10 hrs

"On foot? You're joking."
Andy was aghast, the very suggestion of patrolling a foot beat
sending a shiver down his spine. Apart from his probation,
Andy had spent most of his six years' service avoiding foot
patrol like the plague. In his view it had no place in modern
policing. Ham agreed but thought that was modern policing's
loss not his.

"Don't worry. I won't get lost. I've done this before you
know."

"Yes. But not for twenty years."

"Just drop me off at Woodhouse Park. Pick me up when
you've done the file."

The paperwork for the night's prisoners had been shared
among the shift. Bob McFalls was doing the file for The Alex,
co-ordinating statements from the other officers involved and
charging and bailing all the prisoners. Andy was doing the same
for both visits to Chagrin Avenue. That left Marak Vargo, who
was awaiting psychiatric evaluation, and Booger Smith, who
hadn't committed any offences. Ham could knock out his statement in half an hour but in the meantime he needed some
space. The night had been non-stop, rushing headlong from
one disaster to another. It was indeed the modern way of policing and it was as much Ham's loss as the Police Force's.
Some called it fire brigade policing and that was an apt description. Patrolling your beat had gone out of the window,

replaced by emergency calls and response times. Even the call-centre had ticky boxes to fill in and targets to meet.

The job had come a long way since Ham joined and the journey was downhill all the way. He felt a tightening across his chest and the beginnings of a headache. The anger that had spilled out at Chagrin Avenue was just a symptom not the cure and hadn't relieved the pressure building inside him. He needed to be alone. To return to simpler times, happier times, just as Trevor Garner would like to relive his early days. For Ham that meant patrolling on foot.

The police car cut through the night, heading for the cobbled hillside of Woodhouse Park. The old part of town was the nearest to what Ham remembered when he joined, all terraced houses and slate roofs. They had moved on from outside toilets but the middins were still there, cubbyholes for the dustbins and shelter for the cats. Andy pulled up at the top of the street and Ham got out. He put his coat on and buckled the belt over it. The baton was heavy at his hip but the gas was empty and the radio quiet. A sea of rooftops spread out below him, stretching all the way to the park at the bottom. The trees were dancing in the wind but he couldn't hear them up here. The warmth of the evening had turned into the chill of night and dawn hadn't touched the horizon yet. Ham wanted to walk in the dark one last time.

"Try not to lock anyone else up. I don't like leaving you on your own."

Concern showed in Andy's eyes and Ham felt a touch of sadness.

"Don't worry. I'm over twenty-one."

The concern stayed, not for a lone officer patrolling on foot, but for a friend who was torn inside. Andy wished they'd been able to talk about Ham's problems but was secretly glad they hadn't. What advice could he give to a man almost twice his age?

"Chin up and flies down," was all he could come up with, then he was gone.

*

Once the squeal of Andy's departure faded Ham leaned on the railings and looked across the valley. Dim orange streetlamps picked out the backstreets of Woodhouse Park, throwing the rest of the hillside into stuttering darkness. The moon broke free of the clouds, painting the slates with its pale blue brush. He stood there for a while, soaking up the atmosphere. It was peaceful at this time of night, quiet in a way you couldn't appreciate sitting in a patrol car. The world was asleep and, apart from the occasional dog barking, the night was silent. It was a sound he loved.

After a few minutes he turned towards the street. The houses were tight to the pavement, linking arms like only terraced houses could. Every second house had an alley leading to the backyard and Ham walked down the nearest, enjoying the stillness once you entered the dark. The wind stopped and even the moon was blocked out. Apart from the square of light at the far end he could be in the twilight zone. Walking back through time into his early years.

He arrived at the middin, a stone outhouse that had once housed the outside toilet. Two overflowing dustbins stood beneath its flat roof and a cat stared from its place on the wall. The light round the back came from intermittent flashes of moonlight, picking out the shiny red bricks then plunging the yard into darkness. Across the wall, Ham could see the rear windows of the next street. The curtains were open but the houses in darkness, no lights illuminating the worlds on the other side of the glass. He was glad. He'd seen into too many worlds tonight and it was a pleasant change for the windows to be closed to him.

Back in the days of his probation, when the radio wasn't God and initiative was still encouraged, Ham had walked endless streets during the night. He wore a heavy-duty cape, an item of uniform no longer available, and the heavy black folds hid a thousand secrets. Some bobbies kept sandwiches and a flask under there. Most carried a torch. Barney Koslowski once told him about an ex-telephone engineer who wore a utility belt under his cape, unable to accept that he'd never be able to fix another line or climb another telegraph pole. Maggie kept a full range of make-up accessories under hers but she was the exception. Policewomen in those days looked more like rugby players and were likely to carry gum-shields instead of eyeliner.

Ham cut through the passage into the next street, walking down a wormhole to another era. The streets of Woodhouse Park were still cobbled, succumbing to tarmac on the main roads at the edge of the estate. A broad staircase ran down the hill through the middle of the houses, crossing cobbled streets at each level. Halfway down each drop stood a single lamp, converted from its original gas to electricity but retaining the ornate stand and shade. Ham felt as if Jack the Ripper could walk out of the past at any minute.

He turned right and walked along the street. As he passed each house he looked through the window. Each one was dark but their shadowy interiors spoke of lives untouched by his passing. People he would never meet. There were televisions, and radiograms, and shelf upon shelf of books and magazines. The people who lived there were sleeping and dreaming in the darkness. It made him feel lonely.

Radiograms? What made him think of radiograms? Most of the residents today wouldn't even know what a radiogram was. He remembered the Ferguson radiogram his father owned. It was the family pride and joy. Not only could you tune in for *Sing Something Simple* with The Mike Sam Singers but you could play records ranging from granddad's 78s to the modern 45s and long-players. Tape recorders hadn't changed to cassettes yet and Ham's father couldn't afford a reel-to-reel.

One night, when his parents were out, Ham replayed World

War Two on the carpet and swung his feet too fast. The radio-gram leg snapped off, tipping the cabinet onto the floor. He raided his piggy bank and left fifteen shillings and a letter on the fireplace. When his parents came home he hid under his pillow waiting for the beating that didn't come. No slipper that time but his pocket money was stopped for six months.

He stopped at the top of the steps and looked at the lamp halfway down. It wasn't Jack the Ripper who drifted out of the past. It was Angela. The back-to-back she'd lived in was just like the terraced houses of Woodhouse Park and it was her radiogram that had pricked his memory. It wasn't so much a radiogram as a reproduction that housed a modern hi-fi. That hi-fi reminded him why he wanted to walk for a while and why he had chosen Woodhouse Park to patrol. It was the nearest thing to stepping back in time and the best place to make his decision.

Clouds raced across the sky, bringing the threat of rain ever closer, and blotted out the moon. The blue-grey rooftops blinked out as if someone had turned off the light and Ham stared at the gas lamp. He remembered what Angela had told him on the park bench all those years ago.

*

"I'm sorry for what I've done. It's not your fault." Ham felt tears welling in his eyes.
"Don't do this. Don't end us."

His mind raced, bouncing off any possibilities like a pinball. What could be so bad that she was certain he would finish with her? What other secrets did her past hold? The clue was in her words. "You being a policeman and everything." It must be something his sense of rightness would find offensive.

He remembered how shy she was the first time they'd made love. Even with the lights off she remained almost fully clothed, something he found appealing and a little quaint. The memory threw up another possibility however. A darker one.

Sexual abuse was a terrible thing and could account for her reluctance in the early stages. But no, he discounted that. Victims of such horrors would take much longer to overcome their trauma. And it wouldn't necessarily drive him away. If anything it would make him more protective.

Another thought crept in on the back of that one. She was shy to begin with but quickly developed into a sexual tigress, taking the initiative at every opportunity. The only thing he could think of that might drive him away would be… His mind froze. He could not imagine that would be the case. It wasn't in her nature. Even so, it was the only thing he could think of. Maybe she had been forced into it? Driven to prostitution by family needs.

He hardened his heart. If he found the bastard who'd done that to her Ham would lose his job rather than let him get away with it. A wave of affection welled up inside him. If that was the worst she could come up with then they were saved. He would help her come to terms with it, not abandon her.

Angela took a deep breath, looked down at her feet, and spoke.

"I used to be on drugs… for nearly ten years."

Her words took Ham by surprise. Drugs hadn't even crossed his mind.

"Drugs… like what? Painkillers and stuff?"

Angela shook her head, finding it difficult to speak.

"Then what?"

He thought he knew and his heart sank.

"Cannabis at first. Then Heroin."

Ham felt as if he'd been punched in the stomach. All the strength went out of him. Heroin? Even during his short time in the police he'd encountered drug addicts, sad looking individuals with no life, no energy, and no reason to go on. They were scrabbling for a living at the bottom of the food chain, shackled by a habit that was all invasive. Many died young; alone; murdered by their addiction, the dark twin that flourished inside them. Angela was one of these? He felt sick.

How could that be? She looked so... normal. So full of life. Her words replayed in his head. "...used to be on drugs." Hope re-surfaced, the optimist in him clutching at straws.

"Used to be?"

"Yes. I'm clean now. Have been for six months."

Ham felt like laughing. He pulled her towards him and hugged her.

"Look. The past is the past. Whatever you've done, or taken, or anything, is done. Tomorrow's what counts. Did you really think I'd dump you because of something that's finished with?"

Words from a song in his childhood drifted into his mind. *"Do you think I would leave you dying, when there's room on my horse for two?"* Rolf Harris didn't make him cry but the thought of leaving Angela to die did. Tears ran down his cheeks at the thought of her pain. What she must have suffered to be on the stuff in the first place. He knew about her family, about being abandoned by her father, beaten by her mother, and robbed by her brother. The scars ran deep but he hoped to be the shoulder she could lean on. Not Heroin.

Angela cried too. His shirt was wet with her tears as she promised to stay clean in future. Ham accepted her promise, proving just how naïve he was. An apple could promise not to fall off the tree but gravity would do it every time. Angela fell off the tree twelve months later and Ham's work began in earnest.

*

Ham's problem was twofold; firstly he knew nothing about drugs or the behaviour of its addicts, and secondly he wanted to believe Angela was off them even when he suspected she was not. Most of the time he simply believed she had a cold, or had caught a virus, or was run down because of her family's antics.

Once, when Angela's mother had forced her into care for

unruly behaviour, the old dragon had spread the rumour that Angela was on the game, spreading sexual diseases as frequently as sexual favours. The fact that she'd been taken into care so that Janice could bully Spencer, Rache and Susie never came out. When the social workers admitted their mistake it was too late, Angela's siblings had taken enough punishment for the damage to be done. Angela never forgave the establishment, or the neighbours who had believed the lies her mother told. Later, when she was moving in with Ham, the rumours started again. They slithered through the backstreets like a disease and were whispered to Angela by the few good friends she could muster. There weren't many. The source of the lies was obvious, as was the reason for them. Janice couldn't accept that something was going right for her daughter.

The house was bought and signed for. Angela was decorating it after work and Ham helped between shifts. One night he arrived at the house to find paint sprayed in vicious slashes across the living room walls. The paper scraper was stuck in the door like a knife in the back. Angela was crying on the stairs.

"That miserable bitch."

"What's she been saying now?"

Ham needed no introduction to the machinations of Angela's mother. She was the original wicked witch of the north, as evil as they came and twice as ugly. It amazed him that anyone as beautiful as Angela could come out of someone so foul. Angela told him about the latest rumour and he felt momentarily guilty. Hadn't he considered the same thing when she'd confessed her drugs history? He held her on the landing and kissed away her tears. Angela smiled a sad little smile.

"You know why she's done it don't you?"

"Because she was born from the bowels of the earth?"

"She can't stand to see me happy. Wants to drive you away. This is supposed to send you packing."

"Well, she's sadly mistaken isn't she? Same as you were. Why does everybody think I'm just going to walk away because of a shady past? Whether it's true or not?"

"What would I do without you?"

"You'll never know."

That incident was another nail in the coffin of Angela's self-confidence. Drugs were her coping mechanism because her self-esteem was nil. In her youth, when her mother was lying, and her brother and sisters being beaten, Angela simply couldn't cope without a little help. When the family she had protected turned on her as well she needed more help and before long it wasn't help it was a necessity. She was an emotional cripple and couldn't walk without her crutches.

The first time Ham saw her stoned he thought she was dying. She came home flopping like a boned fish, barely making it through the door. Her eyes were so vacant there didn't seem to be any life behind them at all, the pupils mere pinpricks in the pale blue irises. She was as white as a ghost. He hit the roof when he realised what was wrong with her and slept on the settee. She tried to calm him down, professing her love for him with great slobbery kisses that made him feel sick. He couldn't stand her touch and sent her to bed.

There were long periods of domestic bliss but sooner or later there would always be another fall from grace. The apple fell off the tree because that's what apples do and Ham grew increasingly impatient with her promises. She claimed to be clean and appeared to be just that but truth be known she was never without drugs of some kind. Angela still looked beautiful. The ravages going on inside her body had little effect on the outside. Okay, she looked pale sometimes, and suffered from occasional outbreaks of spots but he assumed they were period spots when she was rundown. With a little effort he could make himself believe anything because that's what he wanted to believe. He loved her. It just wasn't enough.

The house began to fall apart, slowly at first. When they'd moved in they both spent hours cleaning, and decorating, and furnishing it. It was clean and tidy in the way a newly-weds' house should be. They weren't married but that wasn't important. They were happy. Washing up was the first sign, then the clothes. Neither liked to see the cups and plates left after dinner but soon Angela stopped doing her share, leaving half finished meals on the table for hours. Ham usually washed them when he came in, but after a late shift it was the last thing he wanted to do.

The night she couldn't feel her legs he almost called an ambulance. He finally realised just how bad Angela was but she wrestled the phone from him.

"I'll be all right. Give me time. I'll be all right."

Ham wasn't convinced. While she spent the night thumping her thighs to get feeling back in her legs Ham paced the kitchen, wracked with indecision. She made him promise not to call.

"It just slows my body down. Honestly. Don't call."

She slept like a dead person. That was the problem. Ham didn't know if she was a dead person. Her skin became pale and waxen, cold to the touch, her breathing so shallow it was almost non-existent. He nudged her every hour to make sure she was alive. It was the longest night of his life. His mind raced, weighing the promise against her need for hospital treatment. He felt guilty, and weak, and humiliated. How could he tell anyone about it?

That was the worst thing, not how bad she was, but his selfish worry about how to tell his parents? Moreover, as a policeman, how do you tell your colleagues that your girlfriend's a drug addict? It was that selfishness that made him feel guilty. When Angela was so poorly, how could he feel sorry for himself?

Still he pushed the worries aside. Believing what he wanted to believe, that this was only a weaning off period while she settled into her new life with him. There was no stress between them, nothing for her to worry about; surely things could only get better? The glass was half full after all.

He didn't realise until later that the glass was almost empty.

There were no more nights when he thought she was dead,

because instead of coming home late, she stopped coming home at all. On those nights Ham composed his leaving speech, promising to deliver it when he saw her again. The first couple of times when she didn't return, he worried until his mind shut down and forced him to sleep. On a couple of occasions it was two days before he saw her again and when she finally dragged herself home she looked like the addict she was. It broke his heart to see the woman he loved looking so completely wrecked.

The house became a rubbish tip. She had neither the will nor the energy to clean up after herself and despite promises to tidy up she never did. The kitchen was awash with make-up, abandoned clothes, and dirty dishes. Ham continually cleared the work-surfaces, washing the plates because he needed to use them again, but they became cluttered whenever she was around.

The overnight stop-outs became two-night layovers, and the two-night layovers became regular occurrences. Over the years Ham stopped composing leaving speeches and began formulating obituaries, mental notes on how to tell his parents that his girlfriend had died of a drugs' overdose. It began to play on his mind that he might actually be better off if she did die, because he could never leave her. To leave her was to sign her death warrant.

"I don't know what I'd do without you," she often said. "I think I'd end it all."

Ham didn't start worrying about her until she'd been missing for at least two days, and at its worst he contemplated the funeral even before the death. The relief he felt at her passing would only be surpassed by his grief, and his grief only surpassed by the guilt at feeling relief. Whenever she returned he felt sadness and joy. Sadness that it was all to do again, and joy that she was alive.

It was the first time she stayed out for three nights that finally forced his hand. On that night he actually phoned the hospitals, checking under her name and his – she'd taken to calling herself Habergham to escape the family she detested. She wasn't there. He should have been relieved but the fact that she hadn't made it to hospital only made him more concerned. He imagined her collapsed in some crappy flat surrounded by used needles.

Work was a nightmare. Ham was unable to concentrate for more than a few minutes at a time. Somehow he muddled through the day, certain something bad had happened, and when he found her in the kitchen after work the tension finally exploded. He smashed cups, tore up her magazines and threw a teaspoon at the pantry door so hard that it stuck handle first. He swore at her, threw her clothes down the stairs, then hugged her until he cried. He couldn't cope with it any more and told her so. She would have to do something about it or find somewhere else to live.

After a lot of phone calls, most of which left him close to despair, he secured an appointment with a sympathetic doctor, and Angela's road out of the dark began. Ham accompanied her to every meeting, despite the embarrassment of sitting in secret corridors with drug addicts far worse off than Angela, and shouldered the burden of keeping her on the straight and narrow. Six months later she declared herself clean and he was so happy that he married her the following week. He loved her and couldn't see life throwing anything worse at them. The new-found legitimacy would give her stability and a solid foundation on which to build a new life. Ten years had already flowed under the bridge. Surely the next ten years could only get better.

*

The wind strengthened, blowing the mists of time from his tired brain. He stretched his back and patrolled the cobbled streets, walking down a corridor of time that was calming and pleasant. He found himself whistling the theme from *When The Boat Comes In*, and smiled at the thought of his sergeant trying to catch him out. At the time crossing your sergeant was tantamount to snubbing God. It seemed insignificant now, the passage of time washing the slate clean.

Ham wished something could wash the second ten years clean but married life had proved no better than single life with Angela. One way or another her family managed to stick the knife in and every time they did Angela fell off the tree again. The house, after an initial burst of cleaning, got worse and Ham's despair grew tenfold. Twice Angela got clean by herself, using methadone purchased in town, and twice she failed. Ham led her through the rehab clinic one more time then gave up on her.

They didn't so much live together as exist together. It was an existence he could no longer tolerate. Walking barefoot through the house before coming to work he scrunched his toes on the broken peanut shells and vowed he'd had enough. And that was it in a nutshell; a broken nutshell was the straw that broke the camel's back.

Ham thought about the people whose lives he'd visited tonight, the partnerships that were forged in the heat of passion, and the couples who had no reason being together in the first place. The Delbacaros were happy as pigs in shit and would probably last a lifetime. Loren Elkins looked set to renew her allegiance to Peter. Booger Smith was destined to live his life alone and should count himself lucky. And Trevor Garner was stuck between a rock and a hard place, both wives as ugly as each other and likely as greedy. Maybe it was true, men and women didn't belong together.

Ham walked down the steps to the next street, passing under the gas lamp that was no longer a gas lamp, a policeman who was no longer a policeman. Modern policing strategies had no place for the bobby on the beat, yet that was where he felt most comfortable, walking the streets and meeting the public. Even on a cold dark night he enjoyed interacting with the empty streets and darkened windows. This was his world and he was so immersed in it that he didn't notice the shadow fall in step beside him.

It began to rain. The night was almost over and Ham's career with it. The darkness was turning to grey over the eastern horizon, except the eastern horizon was hidden by low scudding clouds that threatened a storm. Taking one step at a time he reached the road just as the hand touched his shoulder.

"Haven't you been listening to your radio?"

Ham blinked back to the present. Andy tapped the handset on his shoulder.

"They've been calling you for ages. We've been given a shit job."

13 Maple Court

"I think I've killed my wife," the voice on the phone said.
For Eric Orbom the tragedy wasn't that he had killed Connie
but that he had failed to kill himself. The pensioner's voice
crumbled.

"Connie's gone."

In the early hours of a cold wet Monday morning, the aftermath of what they had planned was too terrible to contemplate, but during dinner the previous evening the end had already been decided. It was simply a case of tying up loose
ends and they did that together, as they had done everything
together for the last fifty years.

*

"Do you want peas or carrots?"

Connie's voice was cheerful as she called from the kitchen.
Eric sat at the dining table writing the first of three letters in a
steady hand. The smell of roast beef and Yorkshire pudding
drifted through the open door. He hoped she was making the
gravy thick, as he liked it, and knew without asking that she
was. You don't spend half a century with someone and not
know how they like their gravy.

"Carrots please. My eyes are going."

"Your eyes have been going for twenty years."

Eric pushed the bifocals back up his nose and had to agree.

Close up at least. He could see the hair on a gnat's belly at a thousand paces but couldn't see the hand in front of his face close up. Reading the daily paper was difficult enough without his glasses but writing a suicide note was impossible.

"Don't be cheeky, or I'll make you lick the envelopes."

Connie laughed and he paused to listen. She had a wonderful laugh and one he heard too infrequently since the illness. God had granted Eric a fruitful life, giving him good health, a beautiful wife, and fine children, but at seventy-nine he couldn't help thinking it was time to pay for his good fortune. He could have accepted his own health beginning to fail but stealing Connie's vitality was too much to bear. Something he could not bear alone.

"How do you spell that thing that's wrong with you?"

"Pancreatic cancer?"

"Yes, that. How do you spell it?"

Connie spelled it for him. She was four years younger than Eric and after all these years he could still have eaten her up. Perhaps that should be their final act together, making love as only old people can, with sensitivity, and calm, and deep affection. As he tried to concentrate on the letter he couldn't help recalling their life together; with the plans already laid it would be surprising if he didn't. He remembered meeting her at the football match, back when footballs were solid and heavy, not the modern speedballs they used nowadays. If you tried kicking a football that wasn't fully inflated in his youth you would break a leg. Heading one was like heading a brick. His head was built like a brick just after the war and his legs were fairly solid too. It was the legs that attracted Connie.

The match was a ragtag game between the Kirkstall Brewery and the Bridge End Iron Forge. Saturday afternoons were designated sports days and Eric turned out for the brewery every second match. There was no shortage of players and Eric wasn't the best they had but he was still a regular member of the squad. Connie was passing with her sister when she first caught site of those legs. He smelled of barley and hops. When she walked across the tramlines with him later, her sister safely in tow, Connie couldn't get over how tall he was. It was like looking up at a skyscraper with hairy legs. Once again it was the legs that won her over. She discovered his sense of humour later. They married twelve months later against her father's wishes. He confessed his early transgressions so they could start with a clean slate.

One day, when he was fifteen, he'd climbed through the window above the shop door to steal a bicycle, not sure how he was going to get it out. Smudge stood guard outside but was gone when Eric climbed back out. The hand that eased him back to earth also eased him into the police station and a stretch at borstal. It became a standing joke that his school was state approved, something Connie occasionally threw at her father to stir the pot.

Their first home was a one-up-one-down terraced house overlooking the canal. It had no electricity apart from the single bulb on each floor. If they wanted the radio on Eric had to use an adaptor plugged into the light fitting, forcing them to choose between light or music. Candles solved that problem, creating many romantic evenings in front of the radio. When they eventually joined the television age Eric felt they had lost something rather than gained.

The couple's mettle was tested early. After six months Eric was diagnosed with tuberculosis. TB. That was after two months of the doctor telling him he only had a heavy cold and later that he was suffering from hay fever. He was relieved that there was nothing seriously wrong but Connie recognised the fear written across his face. She insisted that he see her doctor who delivered the bad news. Eric was admitted to hospital and found out Connie was pregnant on the same day.

He didn't come out again until eighteen months later.

That wasn't the worst of it. Two months after Connie gave birth to Andrew she was diagnosed as well and rushed into hospital. While surgeons removed one of Eric's lungs and doctors treated Connie with radiotherapy someone broke into their house and stole the radio. The thieves also took a chest of drawers, two jackets, Eric's benefit book, and a packet of Woodbines. He hoped the cigarettes gave them cancer but it was Connie who caught that disease, much later.

Those were truly testing times and they both agreed later that they were their strongest times. When you have nothing but each other, then having each other becomes the glue that binds you together. Connie's only regret was not being able to share her son's first months with Eric, who was fighting for his life in a National Health ward. When he was released, a shadow of the man she fell in love with, he was confronted by a loving wife and a nine-month-old stranger.

That was their lowest point and nothing that followed could even compare. Eric swore that the reason they had such a strong marriage was because their vows were tested while their love was still at its strongest. They had no mid-life crisis because their crisis came at the beginning. Three children and five grandchildren later, Eric became the healthiest one-lunged man any of his family knew; a man with an unquenchable lust for life and a wicked sense of humour. And an undying love for his wife.

They bought the flat at Maple Court when he retired, choosing number thirteen to thumb his nose at the fates that tested him early on. He still had the car, a Ford Fiesta hatchback that Connie loved because she could put her cup in the drop-down tray, and kept a garage underneath the flats to protect it from the elements. He washed it by hand twice a month and waxed it every spring and autumn.

"Those letters aren't going to write themselves."

Connie stood in the kitchen doorway, a steaming pot of vegetables in one hand.

"I hope you're not having second thoughts."

Eric looked at his wife and the pen trembled.

"How could I have second thoughts? You know I can't live without you."

She suddenly grew weak, almost spilling the pan over the carpet. Eric went over, took the pan, and led her into the kitchen. Mouth-watering aromas filled the air, a reminder of so many Sunday dinners and Christmas get-togethers. Connie was never happier than when the family were together and it pained her that they had to leave the family out tonight. Leave them out, apart from the letters Eric was struggling to write.

"Come and sit down for a minute. You need a break. We can't have you ruining the carpet tonight of all nights can we?"

He set the pan on the cooker and turned the gas down to simmer.

"How about a glass of wine?"

Eric brought her a glass of chilled Liebfraumilch and sat at the table with her. He couldn't help thinking how frail she looked, remembering how her sister had been towards the end. Pancreatic Cancer. The curse of her family. It had taken her father and her sister too. Connie nursed Margaret through the early stages and when it became too much she was admitted to hospital. Six months later she was transferred to a hospice and it was all downhill from there. The ravages her sister endured were too painful to recall and yet Connie couldn't help but recall them. There was the immobility first, then the agonising pain, and finally the humiliation of not even being able to regulate her own bodily functions. She died just after Christmas the following year.

The end didn't come soon enough for Connie. Not soon enough for Margaret's dignity to be spared, or the pain relieved. She vowed never to be in that position herself, planning what to do even then if the disease struck her too. But she had only accounted for herself; including Eric was a tough pill to swallow.

"I feel so guilty, taking you from the children too."

"The children are grown up, Connie. They can take care of themselves."

"And the grandkids."

"The grandkids would have to grieve over us sooner or

later. But I can't grieve for you."

They held hands at the table.

"Go see to the dinner or you'll burn the meat. I've got these letters to finish."

Connie stood up, feeling stronger than when she sat down, but no less sad. She went into the kitchen and prepared the last dinner. Their very own last supper. By the time she brought it in Eric was on the last letter. There was a neat pile of documents beside the envelopes, deeds for the flat, insurance policies, TV licence, and the car registration book. He set them aside while they ate dinner and helped with the washing up. Once that was done he sealed the envelopes, put a rubber band round the documents, and laid them in the middle of the table.

"I'll put the hot water bottle in the car later."

Connie nodded, sitting on the settee in front of the fire. Eric turned the radio on and dimmed the lights, just like old times, only different. He brought another bottle and two glasses and they sat arm in arm until it was time.

*

It was dark when Eric woke up. And very quiet. There was no familiar ticking of the bedside clock and no comforting sound of Connie's breathing. The room was warm and his throat hurt. He must have been sleeping with his mouth open, something Connie always told him about.

"One of these days you're going to catch a whole nest of flies in that mouth."

He smiled at the memory. You could rely on Connie to get straight to the point, one of her pet hates being that if he slept on his back his mouth automatically dropped open. The snoring that followed would keep her awake for hours unless she nudged him onto his side. The mumbled "Sorry," came with closed eyes and very little thought.

As he came awake he tried to turn over in bed but couldn't

and realised he was sitting up. In fact this didn't feel like the bedroom at all and he began to wonder if he'd fallen asleep on the settee. *Yes, that's it. Connie's gone to bed and left me on the settee.*

The night before resurfaced in his mind, scattered images like a broken jigsaw; the romantic cuddle by candlelight, the soft music, and the two glasses entwined into a loving cup. It was hard to imagine a more perfect evening, taking him back to their early days in the one-up-one-down. Those were truly their hardest times, and their finest moments. He found himself thinking of them more often just lately, a sure sign of old age. Nostalgia for the past only proved how far away the past had become.

The night was very dark, no light at all filtering into the living room. Eric waited for his eyes to adjust and began to panic when they didn't. For a moment he was certain he'd been struck blind in his sleep. Particles of light slowly seeped into the room, strange lights he didn't recognise, then he realised he wasn't in the living room at all. That threw up a brief moment of fresh panic. Nothing seemed familiar; the only light a dim red glow in front of him.

There wasn't total silence. An intermittent ticking, like cooling metal, licked at his ears. And there was a smell too. Like the time they'd run out of petrol in a tunnel near London. Eric had walked to the entrance with his one-gallon can, almost being overcome by exhaust fumes. They gave him a headache and burned his throat. Eric sat bolt upright. Made his throat hurt? And a headache? He realised that his head felt thick and heavy, a dull ache pounding at his temples. He recognised the smell now; definitely exhaust fumes. The rest of the evening fell into place, the letters, the documents, and the peaceful cuddle that signalled the end.

He remembered starting the car in the garage and putting the hot-water bottle on the passenger seat to warm Connie's back. The vacuum hose was difficult to fit over the exhaust pipe but he managed it eventually, squashing it slightly when he closed the hatchback on it.

The red battery light flickered on the dashboard, illuminating his legs and hands. It reflected off the windscreen and painted the interior with an eerie glow. Eric turned, his neck stiff, and looked into the darkness that was the passenger seat. Slowly, painfully slowly, his eyes adjusted, first picking out the glint of red on the door handle then the pale upholstery of the headrest.

Finally he saw the sleeping face of his wife, still and silent, and knew she wasn't sleeping at all. She was at peace. Outside it started to rain.

*

"Watch out."

Ham's warning almost came too late as Andy swung the car into Maple Court. The entrance swept down towards the parking bays in front of the flats, bordered by neatly trimmed lawns and massive trees. The man they nearly ran over staggered against the garage wall. His eyes were glazed and Ham's heart sank. *Not another drunk please. Not tonight.* The last night of the week was littered with beer-in-brains-out merchants and Ham really didn't feel like dealing with another one so late in the shift.

Andy skidded to a halt, doing better than the last time Ham witnessed a near miss. That hadn't been a near miss at all, Andy knocking down a bottle-wielding hooligan outside a pub fight. The dent on the bonnet took two days to hammer out while the dent in the hooligan took no time at all. Being completely pissed had relaxed him so much he didn't feel a thing.

It was raining hard now and the old man was soaked but he didn't seem to care. He recognised the uniform when Ham got out of the car, waved with an unsteady hand, then almost fell over. Ham grabbed his arm and led him under the flat roof over the entrance. As soon as he touched him Ham knew he wasn't drunk. The eyes looked confused and he was unsteady on his feet but there was no smell of alcohol on his breath. The old man's speech was clear, if slow, and Ham realised this was the man they'd come to see.

"I think I killed her. Connie's gone."

His eyes weren't glazed they were streaming tears.

"What's your name please?"

First things first. Eric told him while he leaned against the wall. And his age. Seventy-nine. How that number kept cropping up tonight. Blue light splashed his face, lightning strikes from the police car parked in the drive. Some calls demanded leaving the lights on. This was one of them. They would act as a homing signal for the other units.

"Eric. Are you all right standing or do you want to sit down?"

Ham thought the old man was going to collapse but he shook his head. A smell Ham didn't recognise came off him in waves, faint but definitely there. He made a mental note. It might be important later.

"Where is your wife?"

"Connie."

"Yes. Where is Connie?"

Eric pointed then started for the corner of the building so quick that Ham thought he was trying to get away. The old man was round the corner before Ham realised he was leading him to the row of garages beneath the flats. The up-and-over door of the second garage was partly open and Eric pushed it up.

The heat was the first thing Ham noticed, followed by the smell. Stronger than the smell coming off the old man but definitely the same. Exhaust fumes. At first Ham didn't understand. The garage was dark, the only light coming from the streetlamps on the main road, but he could see the back of the Ford Fiesta hatchback. Before Ham could stop him the old man opened the passenger door then fell back against the garage wall, his energy gone.

"Come on. Out in the fresh air."

Ham guided him outside just as Andy came round the corner.

"Ambulance is on its way."

Andy had a better grasp of what was going on. Just because the caller said he thought he'd killed his wife didn't mean she was dead. Ham nodded towards the old man.

"Look after him a minute will you?"

He turned back to the open door. It was time to find out if she was dead. The garage was dark, the walls just redbrick squares criss-crossed with cement the builders hadn't skimmed off. The rough edges snagged on Ham's coat. With the car door open its interior light bled into the garage, picking out a section of wall and a row of shelves. Several coffee jars filled with screws and nails stood on one shelf, each neatly labelled with its contents. Bottles of screen-wash, anti-freeze, and car polish lined the other.

It was so hot in the garage that Ham began to sweat, reminding him how warm it was at the start of the night, a lifetime ago. Rain was teeming down outside and Ham glanced at the old man's silhouette as Andy guided him under the overhanging door for shelter. Ham wished he'd let Andy check the body but wasn't sure he could cope with the old man's grief tonight. The midnight hours had ruined so many lives.

He turned to the car again. He couldn't make out the colour in the gloom but the upholstery was charcoal grey velour, indicating that the car was top of the range. When he ducked down to look inside he wasn't surprised to find that the interior was as tidy as the shelves. Two neatly folded dusters sat on the dashboard shelf. There was a pair of driving gloves, sunglasses, and matching notepads in the driver's door pocket. The carpets were spotless. It was only the pair of legs jutting into the passenger footwell that broke the orderly pattern.

Ham couldn't put it off any longer. With rain drumming on the up-and-over door he crouched beside the car and looked into the face of Connie Orbom. She was dead, there was no doubt of that, but he checked her vital signs anyway. His fingers reached out for the waxen neck and touched warm flesh.

He jerked back, banging his head on the doorframe.

Her face showed all the signs of death, sunken eyes, taut white skin, mouth dropped open with slack-jawed ease, but her flesh was as warm as his own. He half expected her to open her eyes and ask what he thought he was doing? Yet the entire body was as stiff as a board, one arm laid casually across her knees while the other held her chest.

Then he remembered the heat of the garage. With the door closed the exhaust fumes had warmed the enclosed space, warding off the chill of death while welcoming death itself. The fumes were still thick enough to make Ham cough and once he'd checked the pulse in her neck he backed out of the garage. He turned his head up into the rain to let it wash the sight from his eyes. He took a deep breath of fresh air.

"She's dead isn't she?"

Ham looked at the old man and nodded.

"I started the car at about midnight, after I had made her comfy. Her back plays her up sometimes. Then I closed the garage door and sat next to her. We were both tired, and..."

He began to cry but forced the tears back.

"I killed her. Oh God, but why am I still here?"

Through the trees Ham could see more blue lights coming towards Maple Court and a few minutes later an ambulance spun into the courtyard. Two more police cars followed, all leaving their lights on to form a crazy disco without music. A paramedic came over carrying his bag. Andy took him to one side and explained what had happened. Ham spoke as kindly as he could.

"I'm sorry. But because of what you've said I'm going to have to arrest you until we find out just what's happened. You understand don't you? I'm very sorry."

The old man was shaking and Ham wasn't sure if he'd heard what he said.

"You do understand that we have to investigate her death don't you?"

"I'm under arrest? Yes I know, but my wife's dead."

"I'm sorry."

199

"My Connie's gone, and you think I'm bothered what you do? I should be with her now. My wife's gone. Oh God."

This time he couldn't hold back the tears, his body collapsing in on itself as he sagged to the floor. Eric's shoulders heaved with great wracking sobs and he cried himself dry. Ham helped him up and walked him to the ambulance where the paramedic carried out a few preliminary tests. Ham sat on the back step, letting the rain run down his collar. As he stared into space he noticed the letter under the rear windscreen wiper. Without thinking he walked over and picked it up then, as an afterthought, closed the car door. Connie sat alone in death, thankfully hidden from view. Ham saw the vacuum hose squashed beneath the hatchback and dropped the garage door to preserve the evidence. Rain immediately tried to wash the address off the envelope so he slipped it into his pocket. The paramedic waved him over.

"He's going to have to come to the hospital. His breathing's bad, and judging from what he's told me, he could have been sucking in fumes for a few hours. Should be dead as well by rights."

"Yes. I think that was the idea."

Andy came over, hair plastered to his head. His collar was turned up in a vain effort to keep dry.

"You going with him? I'll have to guard the scene until SOCO gets here."

Ham nodded, feeling the strain of a night without end. Another car pulled up and Inspector Samson got out. It was time to hand over to the man in charge; their part in this tragedy in three acts completed. Act One had been played out in the darkened garage and Act Two was about to begin. The investigation. Once Eric was in hospital CID would take over until Act Three. Court. Either Coroners or Magistrates. Ham would have a walk-on part in that but for now it was time to leave the stage. Andy could explain everything to the inspector; Ham had had enough. He climbed into the back of the ambulance and closed the doors.

*

Ham had been dealing with dead people for most of his service; car wrecks, industrial accidents, suicides, or plain old sudden deaths. But he had never dealt with someone who had done the killing. He imagined it being very different to this, probably a serious assault gone wrong, a variation of the beer-in-brains-out scenarios he dealt with every week.

Eric Orbom was a different matter. Ham actually felt bad at having arrested him but when it came to deaths you had to plan for the worst and hope for the best. This was shaping up to be a suicide pact, but until the post-mortem Ham had to prepare for the worst. Ninety per cent of domestic murders were committed by one spouse or the other. Being an old man didn't change that. Age brought wisdom for some but if you were a nasty bastard when you were young then you'd likely be a nasty old bastard when you drew your pension. Ham didn't think Eric fell into that category.

They didn't talk during the journey. Ham was tired and the old man would have found it difficult talking through the oxygen mask. The paramedic monitored Eric's vital signs, making notes as best he could in the swaying ambulance. The old man lay quiet on the stretcher, hands folded across his chest. Occasionally he glanced over, making Ham feel uncomfortable. He felt like he should be making soothing comments like, "Everything will be all right," or, "It's all right, we'll be at the hospital soon." But he didn't say anything. Words were inadequate and probably not true anyway.

Still, the old man kept looking at him. After a while he lifted one hand off his chest and pointed. Ham didn't know where because the finger wavered all over the place, pointing at the roof one minute and the floor the next. Ham sat in the chair, lap strap tight across his thighs. Eventually Eric pulled the facemask down.

"Letter."

It was the only word he got out before a coughing fit seized him. The paramedic cleared his airways and replaced the mask but the single word jogged Ham's memory. He fished the envelope out of his pocket and the old man nodded for him to read it. *To Whom it May Concern* was written in a neat hand across the front. Ham knew whose handwriting it was. The envelope wasn't sealed, the flap simply tucked in like a birthday card, only this was a deathday card.

He didn't want to open it, shouldn't have picked it up in the first place really, destroying any fingerprint evidence there might be. It should have been photographed in situ then popped in a bag for examination later. The letter and its envelope would be photocopied for reading and then the paper ninhydrin tested for latent prints. Ham was past caring tonight and slid his finger under the flap. He pulled out a single sheet of pale blue Basildon Bond with the same neat writing on it. A nod from the facemask encouraged him to read.

To whom it may concern,

I have written this letter in order to explain what has happened and apologise for any distress this may cause whoever finds us. My name is Eric Orbom, from 13 Maple Court. My wife is Connie Orbom, and she has recently been diagnosed as having pancreatic cancer. She has only three months to live. Connie nursed her sister through the same illness and has no wish to die in pain and without dignity as she did. I have agreed to help her die as she lived, in peace and with love.

We have been married for over fifty years, and I cannot live without her. She is in pain constantly, yet never complains. I want her pain to end. We have done everything together for so long that I cannot let her go alone. I want to be with her always, in death as in life, and that is why you find us here together.

Our affairs are in order, and there is a letter to our eldest son, Andrew, explaining everything. He can inform the rest of our family, and make the necessary arrangements. There is also a letter detailing the financial dispersements for legal purposes. Please call the police and give them this note. Thank you.

Yours sincerely,

Eric Orbom.

The letter was countersigned by Connie Orbom. Ham glanced at the man who had killed his wife; unable to grasp the pain he must be feeling, not from the exhaust fumes that killed her but from the fact that he must now live alone. The old man tried to take the mask off and speak again but Ham laid his hand back across his chest.

Later, talking to the doctor while he waited for CID, Ham found out just how ironic Eric Orbom's plight was. He had chosen a form of suicide that was now all but impossible, sitting beside his ailing wife as the poisonous fumes did their work. Except the poisonous fumes weren't poisonous any more. Modern safety features introduced to prevent pollution also prevented the suicide pact from succeeding and separated the couple who had been inseparable for over fifty years.

Unleaded petrol isn't as toxic as the kind in use when Eric started driving. The Morris shooting brake they owned as a courting couple might have done the job but a three-year-old Ford Fiesta was too safe for his own good. The catalytic converter kicked in twenty minutes after Eric started the engine, reducing exhaust emissions by two-thirds. That, added to the cleaner fuel, saved the old man, condemning him instead to a fate worse than death, a life without Connie.

Before Ham was relieved he had one more embarrassing duty to perform, seizing Eric's outer garments for forensic examination. The amount of exhaust gasses trapped in the fibres would determine how long he'd been in the car before the engine cut out. It was more painful than arresting him. Ham put the old man's jacket, trousers, and slippers in separate bags. They would be labelled later but for now it was enough for them to be sealed.

"Can I have my own pyjamas?"

"Where are they?"

"In the airing cupboard at the top of the stairs."

"I'll see what I can do."

Ham didn't think Eric would be allowed anything from the flat until SOCO determined it wasn't part of the crime scene. Murder might be putting it a bit strong but assisting a suicide was still an offence. A nurse brought Eric an open-backed hospital gown.

"Are you going to charge me?"

Ham tried to avoid the question but couldn't bring himself to play it for laughs. Being charged for the hospital gown might have seemed funny with Booger Smith but this wasn't a case where the Soggy Bottom Boys could be any help. No singing in the ward tonight.

"We'll get the pyjamas as soon as we can."

"You know what I mean. You might have arrested me, but Connie is gone."

"At least she's not in pain any more. At least there's that."

"Yes. But I should be with her. Without her I am... nothing."

"I'm sorry."

"You had better set a short date for bail, because I won't be around long."

Ham wanted to ease the old man's pain but what could he say? He tried to think how he would feel if he lost the love of his life instead? That focussed things in a hurry. Ham had been contemplating the end of their relationship all night but it wasn't until now that he considered what life would be like without Angela.

When his father died Ham felt lost, the rudder that guided

him no longer there. From childhood to manhood the one constant in his life had been family and the head of that family was his father. Ham loved his mother, and it was a tragedy when she died, but his father was the guiding light that kept him off the rocks. A lighthouse on the cliff-top of life. Without him Ham felt insecure; rolling in the driver's seat just like the night of the ditch. He had driven too fast and without the belt had lost control. The car skidded off the road and almost killed him. Without his father he had no seatbelt, rushing through life out of control. There was a six month period when he could have gone off the rails altogether if it hadn't been for Angela.

She curbed his drinking and returned him to the straight and narrow. She steadied his ship, becoming the rudder he had lost. She had set aside the problems in her own life to comfort him. He had lost his family, whereas Angela's had abandoned her. His was gone forever while Angela's kept rearing its ugly head to disrupt their life. Ham was convinced that she would have been clean of drugs years ago if Janice, or Spencer, or Rache hadn't kept twisting the knife in the wound.

He looked at the old man, trying to picture himself lying there at seventy-plus. Wondering what it must be like after fifty years of marriage to suddenly lose your right arm? And he had to admit that Angela was his right arm.

Ham felt a sea change coming. Although the things Angela had done upset and annoyed him he hardened his will against them. If they could survive the next four years he would retire and be able to give her his full attention. She only fell off the tree so regularly because her inner strength had been eroded by years of hard knocks and setbacks. It was time for him to help rebuild that strength.

A plan began to form in his mind and as it took shape he didn't know why he hadn't thought about it before? The main problem was Angela's family. The family could only get at her because they knew where she lived. With the lump sum from his pension he could afford to move away, leaving the site of her childhood behind. He had no ties here except for Angela.

It was time to take the ball and run. Just four short years. They could manage that.

His mind was made up by the time he spotted Andy leading a detective through the nurses' station. Ham stood with more purpose than he'd displayed all night. And it had been a long night. He handed the bags to the detective, explained what he had done, and prepared to leave. As an afterthought he remembered the letter, fishing it out of his pocket. He wished he'd photocopied it to show Angela because it explained his feelings better than he could himself. He gave it to the detective.

Rain streamed down the hospital windows as dawn painted the horizon. It had been a long hard night and there was paperwork to do before they could go home. Andy swung the patrol car out of the ambulance bay and Ham looked over his shoulder, watching the hospital fade into the distance. After a few minutes he faced front, putting all thoughts of Eric Orbom out of his mind, and settled in for the last ride of the night.

Monday: 06.20 hrs

It was the flowers that sealed Ham's fate. If he hadn't insisted that Andy swing past the twenty-four-hour ESSO station they would probably have been all right. The rain had stopped by the time Andy swung onto the brightly lit forecourt, an oasis of light in the gloomy morning. There were no other cars at the pumps but Andy pulled up beside the carwash anyway. Ham dodged water dripping from the broken gutter as he entered the kiosk, ignoring the magazine rack and heading straight for the flower stand. There were only three bunches, one scrawny selection of roses and two bunches of carnations. Angela's favourites were pink carnations and one of the bunches had pink and white flowers. Ham took them to the counter, dripping water all over the floor.

"Have you got any blank cards?"

The girl nodded towards the back of the shop, unable to hide her boredom. Ham leafed through the greetings cards. Water ran down his sleeve. The range of cards wasn't very impressive, varying from cutesy-pie children's cards to overblown sentiment cards. The nearest Ham could find to a plain card was a busty wench in a bikini pouting at the reader and saying, "Open me and look inside." Inside there was a big red kiss and no words. Ham thought the card belonged with the pudding-puller magazines on the top shelf but it was the best they had. At least the kiss was a true sentiment and he could write what he wanted for the message.

"I'll just take these."

"Oh yes? And what have you been up to then?"

The girl perked up at the thought of a little scandal.

Ham didn't have the energy to engage in any banter and simply smiled and paid. The girl dumped the flowers in a carrier bag and dropped the card in beside them. Ham fished it out before it got wet. The girl called after his retreating back.

"I hope she was worth it."

Ham paused in the doorway then looked back.

"She is."

He shouldered the flowers and walked to the car. Andy was looking optimistic. He'd recognised the crisis brewing in his partner during the night and remembered what he'd said about leaving Angela. The flowers showed that Ham might be willing to dig in. That was good. They were meant for each other. It would be a shame if pressure of work forced them apart. Ham placed the flowers carefully on the back seat and showed Andy the card.

"Best I could get."

"I couldn't send a card like that. She'd be sure I was playing away."

"You are playing away."

"No need to advertise it though."

Andy looked over his shoulder.

"I'm sure Angela will like the flowers though. Good on yer, mate."

Ham knew she would like the flowers and intended that she understand what they meant. That he was going to stand by her, no matter how difficult, until she was clean of the drugs and clear of her family. All they had to do before going off duty was complete the files and do a statement about old man Orbom. He nodded forwards.

"Home James."

Andy headed out of the garage, turning left towards Pelham Terrace. It seemed like an age since they'd attended the first call of the night and Ham had already forgotten about Marco

Delbacaro's randy dog and even randier daughters. The car swooped down the hill, crossing Stone Acre Bridge and taking the low road back to the police station.

*

They were passing the latticework of backstreets in the dip when the car hit them. The dark blue Ford Escort shot out of Pelham Terrace and glanced off the patrol car's offside wing, twisting the bumper and smashing the headlight. Ham jerked round as Andy spun the wheel to follow it. A smudge of white on the passenger door flashed past and Ham thought he'd seen it before, a business stencil on a company car. Then it was on the main road and speeding away.

Ham screamed down the radio, giving location and direction. Andy floored the accelerator and gave chase. It was the last thing either of them wanted after such a busy night but they had no choice since their car was damaged. Ham checked his seatbelt, determined not to end in another ditch, and squinted after the departing Escort for the registration number. A thought squirmed around the back of his mind but wouldn't come.

"All units, all units. Alpha two chasing a blue Ford Escort on Hampton Road."

The radio called the cavalry, urgency spicing the early morning drone of the operator's voice. She broadcast speed and direction then waited for an update from Ham. Andy raced through the gears trying to catch up but the Escort was hurtling towards town.

"Shit. This bastard's moving."

His knuckles were white on the wheel.

"It's the same one. I'm sure of it."

Ham tried to remember where they'd been when the other car got away from them earlier, certain it was around here somewhere. The night had been so full he found it difficult to time the calls or place their movements. Andy screwed the engine up to full throttle, the needle climbing the scale. Seventy-five. Eighty. Eighty-five. Ninety miles an hour. The road was straight and low, dipping at the bottom then humping slightly over the river. The Escort was doing ninety-five when it hit the hump, launching itself into a long low glide before hitting bottom twenty-five yards ahead with an explosion of sparks.

"Andy, watch it. Watch it. Oh shit."

The patrol car followed, lurching Ham's stomach into his throat then slamming it down to his backside when they hit the ground. The wheel tugged at Andy's hands but he held firm, swerving slightly before shooting forward. They were catching up. Whatever size engine the Escort had was being matched by Andy's mad fling along the open road. There was no traffic and no obstructions for the foreseeable future. Ham broadcast their position and asked for a traffic car to intercept at the Pendragon crossroads.

The Escort spewed smoke, burning oil like the Belgrano as it sank. The gap was closing. Two hundred yards. A hundred and fifty. A hundred yards. Soon Ham would be able to read the registration plate. He squinted at the yellow rectangle below the hatchback.

Seventy-five yards. Seventy. Fifty yards.

The car suddenly slammed its brakes on, scarring the road with burnt rubber then sideslipped left next to The Wellington Arms. Andy was on it in a flash, decelerating through the gears for traction, then Ham was thrown across the seat as they sped round the corner. The Escort was already turning left at the end of the street, brake lights flashing a warning.

"Alpha Two. We're left, left, left, into Wellington Street."

Ham couldn't remember the street at the end and had to wait until Andy turned left as well.

"Left, left, left, into Wellington Terrace."

"Alpha Two. You're on talk-through. Keep the commentary going."

They were in a small nest of backstreets that either led back to the main road or turned right towards the valley. If the car turned right the narrow country lane would slow it down.

You couldn't do more than fifty without marrying a tree or eating ditch out there. Ham kept his fingers crossed because the speed-humps on Wellington Terrace certainly weren't slowing the Escort down.

Thwump-thwump, bang.

The patrol car hit the first hump doing seventy, bouncing Ham to the ceiling. It was only the seatbelt that stopped him crashing his skull against the bolts holding the blue lights on.

Thwump-thwump, bang.

He leaned forward slightly to ease the contact with the seat.

Thwump-thwump, bang.

He rode the humps like a jockey doing the steeplechase, relaxing his spine to lessen the shock. The Escort hurtled towards the T-junction, showing no sign of slowing down. If it hit the junction at that speed it would be curtains.

"He's doing seventy to the end of Wellington Terrace."

His voice echoed from his radio, repeating seconds later like a bad dream.

"He's not turning. Not turning. Shit."

The Escort hit the last speed-hump off-kilter, bouncing the left wheels higher than the rest of the car. The brake lights came on and the front wheels bit tarmac. Right. The car screeched round the corner, grazing the far wall amid a shower of sparks. The nearside wing mirror rattled on the ground then the car righted itself and sped on. Ham caught sight of the white stencil on the driver's door, three capitals and some smaller writing, but still couldn't make it out.

"We're right, right, right, into Valley Road."

Andy braked, slewed the patrol car round, then accelerated. They missed the wall by a whisker. The Escort was already dropping into the first curve, a short drop then hard left. Sixty-five. The wheels left the ground like a hiccup then took the bend. Andy followed, forcing Ham to scream. A jagged branch reached across the road just above car height and for a moment history replayed itself, the car grounding in the ditch as the branch strangled Ham through the shattered window.

Then they were round the corner as well, Andy dabbing accelerator and clutch as he dropped into a lower gear. This wasn't a straight run any more. This needed a touch more control. The Escort was all over the road, still racing along in top gear, all brakes and accelerator, while Andy kept in third and weathered the bends with ease. Not easy enough for Ham, who spat expletives at every turn, his words bouncing back at him from the radio as they sprayed the airwaves. He hadn't sworn so much since Barney tried to get him to say, "Fuck" when he first joined. Now every other word was "Fuck."

"Sorry Alpha Two. I didn't get that last."

"I said shitty fucking death."

"Repeat please."

"I said he's taken a left."

He couldn't be bothered arguing. There were no more turns on this road for half a mile, then the driver would have a choice of left beneath the railway bridge or straight ahead. Straight ahead was a dead end.

"Approaching Bailey Bridge. That's Bailey Bridge. Stand by."

Both cars snaked through the winding road, keeping pace with each other at fifty-five. The gap was closing but Ham still couldn't read the number. Down into a dip then up over the brow of a hill and there was the bridge, stone-dead masonry coming out of the morning gloom. Wispy tendrils of mist clung to the valleys, spreading across the road from the fields. The end of the road was shrouded in a cold white cloak with only the first three trees visible.

Ham crossed his fingers again. The Escort raced towards the bridge, showing no sign of slowing, and he was certain it would shoot straight ahead. He whispered to himself. "Straight on, straight on, straight on." With each word he flicked one finger out, pointing along the road he wanted the car to take, urging it on. No brake lights. Good. At the last moment the car

braked and swerved left. Ham's heart sank. The Escort wobbled with indecision and the patrol car caught up. Suddenly the
number was visible and Ham shouted it down the radio. He
was so elated at reading it that he almost didn't notice the car
feint left then dart forward. Into the cul-de-sac.

"Right, right, right, into Bailey Avenue. It's pulling up."

Ham unsnapped his seatbelt as the car pulled over to the
right. Andy stopped three-quarters to its left, his headlights
picking out the side of the car. White letters leapt from the
blue door. GSI Alarms. There was a telephone number underneath it. Ham reached for the door handle just as the car shot
forward again.

"It's off again. At speed."

Andy slammed into first and sped after it. Trees came out
of the mist, solidifying then flashing past. As the road narrowed, the left hand kerb gave way to rough gravel, then to
parked cars. The right hand kerb stopped as well, replaced by
a high stone wall bordering Bailey Bridge Cottage. After that
there was only a footpath through the woods. They were going to bail out.

"End of the cul-de-sac. They're going to be on foot."

A monster loomed out of the mist on the left, a great yellow
recovery truck parked opposite the owner's house. Andy
shaded to the right then saw the brake lights come on one last
time. The driver's door opened. Ham yelled down the radio.

"Chasing on foot. Chasing on foot."

It was the last thing he managed to say. He had his door
open before Andy stopped the car, watching the driver lurch
to his right. The patrol car pulled up to the Escort's bumper,
preventing any escape, and Andy unsnapped his seatbelt as
well. He could only open his door halfway and stick one leg
out, struggling to untangle himself from the strap. Ham was
stepping out from behind his door to give chase.

The driver caught them both by surprise. He got back behind the wheel and jammed the Escort into reverse. It shot
backwards, slamming the patrol car back four feet in an in-

stant. Ham couldn't clear his door. It caught him in the chest, wedging him against the recovery truck's counterweight. Pain flared in his back as a fixing bolt knifed into the soft flesh above his kidneys. Three ribs snapped like twigs, shards of bone piercing his right lung. Blood spat from his mouth.

Andy screamed.

The patrol car couldn't go any further, blocked by Ham's open door and the yellow lorry. The Escort squealed, engine racing, then mounted the bonnet on Andy's side. His right leg was caught in the closing door like a wire in a pair of bolt croppers. Something gave and Andy screamed. Ham heard sirens in the distance but couldn't place them. He couldn't relate to anything any more. His mind flashed images across a hazy mindscape. The ditch and the tree branch. The naked woman running around her garden with the shard of broken mirror. Angela kissing him goodbye when he set off for work.

Everything else seemed a bit vague. He couldn't remember the beginning of the shift at all; who was on briefing, what the first call of the night was, how many prisoners he'd arrested. All he felt was a world of pain tearing at his lower back and abdomen. The Escort forced the police car away from the wall, squeezing the driver's door shut on Andy's shattered leg. The back wheels slid towards the lorry, pressing the bolt into Ham's back. He felt faint but refused to let go. Andy needed him. Angela needed him. And the cavalry would be here anytime now.

Ham's door shuddered and he saw the Escort ride up almost onto the patrol car's roof. The blue-light assembly smashed, its lightning flashes blinking out. His eyes were so used to them that his mind pretended they were still flashing, burning into his brain with twenty-six years of memory. He remembered the poor excuse for a blue light that his first patrol car had. The Marina was fitted with a single bulb and rotating mirror inside a blue dome. You'd be lucky to see it at night but during the day a packet of Swan Vestas would give off more light.

The Escort wedged itself between the wall and Andy's door. Screeching metal and spinning tyres filled the night air. The noise almost drowned the sirens playing in the back of Ham's mind. Then the patrol car was nudged sideways and forward as the Escort forced its way back. Ham's door swung free, releasing him, and the bolt tore a hole out of his back you could stick two fingers into. He felt like sticking two fingers up at the driver and in a moment of weakness did just that.

The startled face of the driver was a picture, not because he was shocked at being given the "V" sign by an officer of the law but because that officer must surely recognise him. He tried to duck away but not before Ham got a good look at the garden gobshite he'd spoken to twice that night. The sign on the door made sense now.

GSI Alarms.

Garner Security International.

He remembered where he'd seen the car before. It had been parked in the street behind Trevor Garner's house during the wedding video fracas and it had made off from them near the Delbacaros' after the dog bite call, their first job of the night. First and last. The car had been with them all the time. Ham's legs wobbled and he sagged against the truck. Andy sat motionless behind the wheel and Ham knew he should go help him but had no energy left. The Escort gunned its motor one last time and it climbed the roof to freedom. It hit the ground running, reversing into the fog just as a swarm of blue lights turned into the cul-de-sac.

The final act played out in silence as the sirens faded from Ham's ears. The mist seemed brighter; promising a beautiful day once the sun burned it off, providing an off-white movie screen for the action that unfolded. The Escort tried a Jim Rockford reverse handbrake turn but misjudged it badly. The wheels bit too soon, sending the car sideswiping into the near-est police car. First gear didn't help either, the bumpers en-twined like a hand feeling his collar. The driver couldn't get out, his door jammed against the other car.

215

Two more patrol cars and the traffic unit skidded to a halt and more officers jumped out. Two pulled the passenger door open and dragged the driver out. Ham watched as they hand-cuffed him then noticed a concerned figure sprinting towards him. It was Bob McFalls and he was shouting something in a stage whisper. Ham couldn't make out the words, couldn't make out anything. Even Bob's features were beginning to fade and Ham tried to wave back. The hand he raised was covered in blood and he didn't know where it came from.

More officers followed Bob, shocked into action by what-ever he was shouting. Ham looked across at Andy who was completely still. There was more blood on the driver's door. It looked very red in the brightening day. In fact it was the only colour Ham could see amid dawn's misty white curtain and soon even that became muted. A pastel shade in God's paint box. The running policemen slowed down and daylight washed out all colours.

Soon the only thing Ham could see was the shattered blue light fitting on the patrol car roof and the only thing he could hear was the steady thump of the pulse in his ears. Before Bob reached him even that had gone.

HOME STATION

Villa Habergham

Mick Habergham arrived home at four in the afternoon, relieved that they weren't keeping him in overnight. You practically had to be a corpse to get a hospital bed after dark anyway. Angela was at work. That was both a blessing and a
hindrance because he wanted to give her the message per-
sonally, not with a note attached to a battered bunch of flowers. In fact the flowers weren't so much battered as completely destroyed but he didn't have the heart to throw them
away when the message they gave was so clear. The note put
it into words but the bedraggled spray said more. The
Haberghams might be a bit battered around the edges but at
their heart was a core of steel. Ham needed that steel now.

He had regained consciousness in the ambulance and for a
moment thought time had rewound itself to one of his earlier
trips to hospital, with Booger Smith, or Eric Orbom. Reality
slammed home when the pain hit him and he remembered
Andy screaming as his leg broke.

Andy.

Ham looked round, his head swimming, but of course the
ambulance was a single berth, unlike the caravan at Primrose
Valley where he'd spent so many childhood holidays. He tried
to ask the paramedic where his friend was but his mouth felt
full of cotton wool, reducing his speech to a series of vowels
without any consonants. The world spun around an axis that
was his head and his stomach lurched. He was asleep again

before they reached the emergency room.

The examination slid by in a haze of memory and forgetfulness. He remembered the nurse but forgot the treatment. He remembered Andy and forgot about himself. He remembered his love for Angela and forgot about the anger he sometimes felt.

Ham had started the night with a decision in mind; a decision that once made would change his life forever. In the end the decision had been made for him, but not before he settled on a course of action that would save both Angela and himself. He would stick with her, help her through whatever rehab was necessary, and in so doing preserve the future he needed for himself. All he needed was time, time to spend with her during the early stages, time to take her to the meetings and examinations, and time to watch over her while she healed. Time he didn't have because being a policeman was a full time job.

Time he didn't have until Marty Finnegan, Trevor Garner's stepson, smashed into their car and ended Ham's career. With just four years to go, the back injury was enough to secure early retirement but add to that the shock of seeing his partner's leg crushed and narrowly escaping worse himself, and he was looking at injury on duty awards, enhanced pension, and the chance to grow old gracefully.

Ham felt a pang of guilt. He was being selfish again, forgetting that Andy had been injured as well. Andy Scott had a flourishing career ahead of him and now the doctors thought he might never walk again. Why did there always have to be a payoff? Why did someone have to pay for his good fortune? Swings and roundabouts. Life just wasn't fair.

No, it wasn't fair but it was strange. Unseen hands had been pulling the strings of his future all night, introducing him to the ingredients of his destiny without him realising. It was only when Bob McFalls and Billy Hollis came to see him that the pieces fell into place. The hub of the wheel was Garner Security International. All the spokes met there, one way or another. Marco Delbacaro had worked there as a security guard until one of Trevor Garner's stepsons tried to mess with his daughter. Carla, who had been messing about with her cousin for years under Marco's nose, kept seeing Marty long after her father quit his job. Her mother only suspected after Carla fell pregnant. Not fast thinkers the Delbacaros. Most of Eric Orbom's investments were in property, but a small percentage were with GSI, and it was GSI who alarmed Quarry View Cottage, keeping Loren Elkins safe when her husband was working late.

The strings were being pulled long before tonight though. Marty was only fifteen when Trevor's brother allowed him behind the wheel on the night Trevor got run down. It was Marty not Pat who broke Trevor's legs, a small fact Trevor always overlooked when blaming his brother for his fortunes and misfortunes. Due to the severity of Trevor's injuries Marty was disqualified for ten years straight off and didn't hold a driving licence or insurance for the blue Ford Escort. If he had he might have pulled over in the first place and none of this would have happened.

Swings and roundabouts. What you gained with one hand you lost with the other. It just didn't seem fair that Ham's gain was Andy's loss and that weighed heavy on him as he arrived home, climbed the steps to his front door, and slipped the key in the lock.

*

It took Ham almost an hour before sleep took him. Despite knowing that Angela wasn't due home until seven o'clock his mind half listened for the door downstairs. He had drawn the curtains but it was still bright in the bedroom and his mind wouldn't let go of the events of the night. After most nightshifts he was out like a light the minute his head hit the pillow. Tonight hadn't been like most nightshifts.

He found himself missing the windows already; windows

through which different worlds existed. It was the best part of doing the nightshift, that sense of freedom as you patrolled the darkened streets. Those worlds would still exist without him, he just wouldn't see them again, and that was his personal loss. He would have to concentrate on the world behind his own window instead and wondered what an outsider looking in would see.

At the moment they would see a bunch of bedraggled flowers in a vase on the living room table. A creased card leaned against it. Ham had written it at the hospital. As his eyes began to close he remembered the message.

Our love blooms despite the manure.

They pile shit on us, but we grow stronger...

Ham smiled at the thought of Angela's face when she read it. He looked forward to seeing her. He looked forward to the future. He slept.

LaVergne, TN USA
02 October 2010
199343LV00001B/13/A